HELLO, KITTY

ANNE STEVENSON - YANG

AND
OTHER
STORIES

BUI JONES

First published in the United Kingdom by Bui Jones 2024
Copyright © Anne Stevenson-Yang
Cover illustrations Emily Blundell Owers

Anne Stevenson-Yang has asserted her right under the Copyright,
Designs and Patents Act 1988 to be identified as the author of this work

BUI JONES

buijones.com
Bui Jones Limited Company Number 14823240

Printed and bound in Great Britain by Clays Ltd, Elcograf S.p.A.
A CIP catalogue record for this book is available from the British Library
ISBN 978-1-7394243-0-5

All Bui Jones books are printed on
paper from responsible sources.

Hello, Kitty

Anne Stevenson-Yang is a writer, business commentator and analyst. She lived in China for more than 25 years. She is the author of *China Alone* and *Wide Ride*.

CONTENTS

THE DIVORCE

Taking the bus from the subway terminus to the new section of Shunyi, as Bai Run did every week, was like poling a barge down a river in heavy fog. Outside the bus windows, a pointillist grey smog filmed over the sun and created smeared haloes of light around the streetlamps, which were switched on though it was morning. The dirty air hung like a drop cloth over the buildings on either side of the avenue, so that they appeared in outline, like mountain ranges. Most were steel skeletons, still under construction. Only the blue corrugated fences that surrounded active construction sites broke the monotonous grey of concrete and steel. The whole area smelled of car exhaust and wet cigarette butts.

But Bai Run was on a mission to find the best real estate bargain in the city. For the length of the thirty-minute bus ride, she looked at the scarred landscape and saw possibility. Eventually, not long from now, flowers would be planted, grass would grow, and happy couples – the women in pencil skirts, men in smart Western suits – would walk purposefully from their chic apartments to conveniently located, high-end boutiques.

Bai Run was determined that she would participate in this bright future, and to make sure, she and her husband were getting a divorce. That way, they would become eligible to purchase a unit in one of the new high-rises going up outside the city core. They already owned one commercial apartment in addition to the unit that had been granted them by the institute where Bai Run's husband taught. Since there was a limit of one commercial unit per family, they had to become two families. Bai Run and Zhao Gang told their daughter that the divorce would be on paper only and that they would soon get back together.

Bai Run was in a festive mood on a crisp Wednesday morning as she waited to make the divorce official. Her daughter, Zhao Mei, was waiting at the Civil Affairs office before ten, the designated meeting time with her parents, to serve as a witness to the proceeding. Bai Run arrived shortly afterwards.

"Why the long face, Mei?" Bai Run greeted her daughter.

"Because you're getting a divorce."

Zhao Mei was a sallow woman who, her mother had to keep reminding herself, was now over forty and no longer a girl with her life in front of her. Zhao Mei was thin and wore her long, seldom-washed hair in two sheets on either side of her face, like curtains. Her sleeves were habitually draped over her hands, and she hunched, as if she wanted to disappear into her clothing like an eggplant wrinkling and desiccating in the refrigerator crisping drawer.

"Don't be silly!" Her mother pinched her cheek. "It's just so we can buy an apartment. You know that! And you'll inherit it, so you should be thanking me!"

They were standing in the dusty reception hall of the Civil Affairs office in the East District of Beijing, where Bai Run and Zhao Gang had been married. At ten past, Zhao Gang came limping in. He had an ailment no one could identify that had progressively attacked his right leg, which now hung off him like a sandbag, incapable of independent motion. Zhao Gang would extend his left leg, lean far over so that the right leg pulled up off the ground, and then swing it around and forward like a sack of potatoes. His daughter greeted him warmly. His wife was less enthusiastic.

"We've been here for fifteen minutes," she said, eyeing his clothing. "You could at least have worn a nice shirt."

"A student called me just as I was leaving my office," Zhao Gang said. He was a professor of English at the International Relations Institute. "She needed an extension on her senior paper."

"I'm sure she did," said Bai Run archly. "I wonder why she didn't go to your office to tell you in person." Zhao Mei knew that this was a reference to her father's affair with a student some fifteen years earlier.

Her father ignored the comment and turned to Zhao Mei.

"Work going well?"

"I took the day off," she said. Zhao Mei and her husband

had a small company that distributed medical equipment, mostly older, refurbished X-ray machines. Her husband spent most of his time travelling to sell to hospitals in southern Hebei Province, while Zhao Mei handled the invoicing and accounts. It was a dreary business. Her mother did not approve: the money was meagre since competition was so intense, and the unpredictable ups and downs of the trade made Zhao Mei's days stressful, a situation that upset her mother because she was convinced that stress would make Zhao Mei unable to conceive. Actually, Zhao Mei had told her mother early and often that she did not plan to have a child, but Bai Run forgot this as often as she was reminded.

The three sat for a time on folding metal chairs in the office, occasionally remarking on the other people waiting there. Bai Run had taken a number as soon as they arrived, but there were still more than thirty numbers ahead of them. The clock showed twenty minutes past eleven. Each case was taking at least five minutes, sometimes more, and there were two windows, so they figured the thirty cases in front of them would take over an hour. The office would close for an hour at noon, so the family decided to visit a restaurant down the street for lunch.

Bai Run strode purposefully in front, and Zhao Mei and her father walked behind, talking. They were shown to a small private room with a table that could accommodate eight. The three sat clustered around one edge of the table, facing the door. A waitress turned on a television hanging in a metal bracket in the corner of the room. They ordered lunch.

When the food came, Bai Run tasted a bit of cabbage and made a face. "I make this vinegar-cabbage dish much better than they do. How do they get away with charging thirty-five renminbi for it?"

She flagged the waitress. "Miss! The rice is very dry. You must have served us from a pot you made hours ago. Get us three new bowls."

Zhao Mei lifted her eyebrows and gave the waitress a little shrug. Without complaining, the waitress brought them fresh bowls of rice. She started to leave.

"You haven't refilled our teapot!" Bai Run called to her.

The waitress picked up a thermos from the sideboard and poured hot water into the little pot of tea.

"Does this restaurant charge for napkins?" Bai Run asked her.

"We charge one renminbi for a packet of napkins," the waitress said. She was a ruddy-cheeked girl with a northeastern accent. Zhao Mei could imagine the village she came from, her trip to the city to find a job, her long days at the restaurant, how much she missed home.

"Ridiculous!" Bai Run said. "We should be able to wipe our mouths for free, wouldn't you agree?"

"Run," her husband said quietly. "Can't you just leave her alone? We have to go back to the Civil Affairs office soon anyway."

Bai Run snapped her head around to look at her husband. Her eyes seemed to harden and focus into two black points.

"If I didn't take responsibility for this family, no one would! And I get no gratitude."

"We appreciate you. We just want to have a quiet lunch," Zhao Mei said.

They went back to eating. Presently, a fat tear dropped

into Bai Run's soup.

"Ma! Is it really that bad?"

Bai Run, burning from the reproach, turned her wet cheek to her daughter.

"You always take his side. I am alone in this family. No one ever supports me."

"Ma, you know that's not true."

Zhao Gang focused on spooning up hot-and-sour soup, which he had poured over the rice in his bowl. He spun the lazy Susan to reach the plate of corn grilled with pine nuts and took a scoop. "The corn is really sweet," he said. "It reminds me of autumn back home in Jilin."

"So now you want to go back to your miserable life on the farm?" Bai Run said.

"That's not what I was saying, Run. I just meant to say they do the corn well here." Zhao Gang had a defeated tone that his daughter recognised.

"They add sugar. That hides the stale flavour of the corn," Bai Run said. "I'm surprised you can't tell, you being a farm boy." Farm boy was not a compliment for Bai Run; it connoted backwardness, poverty, ignorance.

It was time to return to the Civil Affairs office. Zhao Gang paid the bill, and they walked the short distance back, not speaking. When they were called to the window about thirty minutes later, they made their statements, and the document was duly stamped. After forty-one years, Bai Run and Zhao Gang were divorced.

Love had never entered the equation for Bai Run, and she would have been surprised to hear that it mattered to anyone. When Bai Run first met Zhao Gang, she was working in far-off Qinghai in the ticket office of the railway station. Zhao Gang was a Red Guard and could take the train anywhere in China without a ticket, supposedly to gain a better appreciation of how the peasants lived, but actually just because he wanted to travel. One night, he had disembarked in Xining, the capital of Qinghai Province and a centre of Tibetan Buddhism. He wanted to see the large temple there, which Tibetans were said to circumnavigate crawling on their stomachs. Local entrepreneurs sold knee pads and rush mats for pilgrims to protect their legs and stomach as they dragged themselves over the hardscrabble earth.

Zhao Gang, then a tall, sturdy young man in a green army jacket and cap, got to talking with Bai Run, who happened to have the next day off, and she agreed to take him to Ta'er Si, which Tibetans called Kumbum. The temple was not operating, then – it was the middle of the Cultural Revolution – but the two walked around and lunched on the hard-boiled eggs and crackers that Bai Run had brought. Eggs were a delicacy then and bringing them showed her special consideration for Zhao Gang. This was not without calculation: Zhao Gang was attending the elite Harbin Foreign Languages Institute, which was operated by the Public Security Bureau, and he had a good chance of being sent to Beijing after graduation. A wife would naturally go with him, and Bai Run desperately wanted to get back to Beijing. For Zhao Gang, a country boy, Bai Run was sophisticated. He was in his mid-twenties, and it was time to marry. Zhao Gang left Xining two days later, but he returned after two months for a week, and by the time he left, he and Bai Run were engaged.

The couple moved to Beijing, where Zhao Gang

had been assigned a job teaching English, and the same institute gave Bai Run a job as librarian. The couple had a daughter in 1976, and the institute sent Zhao Gang on a year-long fellowship to Iowa University, where he was expected to gather information about Americans and their politics. For Zhao Gang and his wife, the posting was an opportunity to salt away some hard currency, and when he returned to Beijing, they acquired a top-of-the-line washing machine.

But that turned out to be the pinnacle of their family's success. Bai Run had started too many feuds with colleagues at the institute to be offered advancement from her position. Zhao Gang was passed over for promotion to department head and eventually dean; it was whispered that he had affairs with students.

And their daughter was disappointing. Zhao Mei had moved out at fourteen to live with her uncle and never returned home. The dispute with her mother that drove her out began because a friend had brought the family a VCR of *La Bamba*, and Zhao Mei had watched it. The film contained a kissing scene, so Bai Run confiscated the cassette and demanded to read her daughter's diary to look for signs of budding interest in sex. Zhao Mei refused to produce the diary. Her mother searched her room when she was at school. She found the diary, broke the flimsy lock, and read that Zhao Mei liked a fourteen-year-old boy in her class. When Zhao Mei got home from school, her mother told her that she would go nowhere but home and school for the next month. An argument ensued, and Zhao Mei ended up moving to her uncle's apartment.

"Why do you have to alienate everyone?" Zhao Gang had asked his wife.

"Someone needs to watch out for our daughter's interests," she retorted. "Clearly, that's not going to be you."

"My mother is just impossible," Zhao Mei told her uncle Bai Li.

The atmosphere in Bai Li's home was more permissive, and instead of cramming for the senior-high exam, Zhao Mei spent her Sundays cycling around the city with a group of friends. She picked up street slang that was then fashionable. After attending a mediocre high school, she managed to get into a technical school in Shandong specialising in hospitality. There, she learned how to operate a cash register and how to greet guests in English, Japanese, and German.

"What is hospitality?" her mother said. "What kind of a profession is that? Zhao, help me here. Your daughter is throwing away her life."

"If that's what she wants," he replied, softly.

"How does she know what she wants?" snapped his wife. "She's a child. We're her parents. We know what's best for her."

"This is a different era, Run," he replied. "Maybe hospitality is the new wave, just what she needs to get ahead."

"What nonsense! Just because it's a different era doesn't mean we can't understand when hotels get together to exploit cheap labour by calling it training." There was some truth to this. "She is going to learn nothing and end up being one of those women who sit in hotel lobbies and do nothing."

Zhao Gang pulled out his copy of the People's Daily.

"How about if we withhold her allowance? She'll have

to leave that school." Bai Run kicked Zhao Gang at the ankle, but he just kept reading his newspaper. In the end, he let her think they had cut their daughter off, but he sent Zhao Mei money every month without telling his wife.

In those years, Bai Run had no daughter at home to care for and tried different hobbies – ballroom dancing, still-life painting, water aerobics – but after a couple of weeks, the old ladies in the classes got on her nerves so she decided not to continue. "It's not as if I can't learn painting on my own," she would say. Bai Run felt that her days were increasingly empty, and ultimately, when Zhao Mei got married and said she did not want to have a child, Bai Run knew her own idleness would be indefinite. It made her wonder the point of everything. She seemed to be looking down a long, featureless tunnel that had only one destination.

Then the property boom came along. Land values began skyrocketing. People who had worked at a white-collar job overseas for a decade and had managed to save RMB100,000 would return to China only to find that they could have stayed there and been worth far more. Family and friends were sitting on gold mines. The value of a dusty little apartment in central Beijing had gone from tens of thousands of dollars to over a million. Not only property: investments were going crazy. Farmers sold their fields to the government and bought "wealth management products" earning two per cent a year. People with no obvious skills suddenly had money. And Bai Run wanted to be one of them.

She knew she had a nose for real estate. An elderly neighbour had left a decade earlier for America and left her apartment to Bai Run, who spent all her savings on the fees required to "privatise" the apartment and make it saleable. The process took two years and patient negotiation. After paying off the loan and giving the old lady's family 50,000 renminbi, Bai Run still had 3 million renminbi. She immediately purchased a "study" apartment in the coveted Haidian District, where ambitious parents hoped to live so their children could attend the best schools, and she spent the whole 3 million renminbi on a 50 per cent down payment. Again, it turned out to be an astute move, since the apartment rose from 6 million to 18 million renminbi in just five years.

That was when she decided she and Zhao Gang should divorce to maximise their wealth. Shunyi was the up-and-coming area, with all the international schools and villa developments for executives of foreign companies. Bai Run was looking at the developments to turn the profit from the study apartment into something truly remarkable. She prepared in military fashion, with the discipline that she found was part of her true nature. Making money was her calling.

After helping them with the divorce, Zhao Mei and her husband, Wang Lu, visited next Sunday.

"Where's my dad?" she said on arriving, seeing none of her father's things in the apartment.

"He's rented a new apartment for a couple of months. The government is cracking down on fake divorces. He thought it would be better for us to make it look as real as possible."

Zhao Mei did not comment.

Bai Run had become someone worth paying attention to. Acquaintances sought introductions. People she barely knew invited her to dinner to learn about investing. She bought a BMW, because, she told her daughter, someone of her stature needed to have a fancy car.

Zhao Mei and Wang Lu were financially unambitious, something her mother found incomprehensible. They lived in a small, dark rental apartment on the South Second Ring Road, and they did not own a car. Bai Run wanted them to think bigger.

"This is the time to buy real estate," she told them over Sunday dinner. "Don't you want to get out of that little apartment and have your own place?"

"Not really," Zhao Mei answered, pressing her lower lip against the rim of her bowl so that she could shovel the last grains of rice into her mouth with her chopsticks. "It's very convenient. What would we do way off in the suburbs?"

"You could buy a car. Then the commute would take you no longer than you spend on the subway now, and without all the crowds."

"So we buy a place that's a lot farther out of town than the apartment we have now, and we have to buy a car to make up for the extra distance."

Wang Lu knew enough to stay clear of the conversation. He studied the food on the table and carefully picked up a jumbo shrimp with his chopsticks and placed it into his mouth. He held the shrimp between his incisors and removed the shell with his tongue, loudly sucking the sweet tomato sauce from the crevices between the joints in its carapace.

"Don't you want to own something? When you pay a mortgage, you are paying yourself, not some landlord."

"We'll think about it, Ma," said the husband to end the topic gracefully.

"I can advance the down payment," Bai Run said, reluctant to drop the subject. Her offer was met with silence. Her daughter was picking at the dumplings as Wang Lu served himself a large bowl of soup. Neither of them asked where Zhao Gang was. Bai Run volunteered, "Your father couldn't make dinner, because he had a departmental meeting."

Zhao Mei knew this was not true; no one held meetings on Sunday.

"He agrees with me, you know," Bai Run continued, imagining that Zhao Gang would also have a keen interest in having them buy an apartment. "He thinks you should stop wasting your money on a rental."

Zhao Mei knew that she disappointed her mother by not having children, not being wealthy, not buying an apartment, not being sunny and agreeable, and the atmosphere of failure made her even more sour. She had married Wang Lu as soon as they both graduated from college, more as refuge from her family's disapproval than a desire to be married.

"Not everyone thinks gaming the real estate market is the purpose of life," Zhao Mei told her mother acidly, picking apart a dumpling with her chopsticks to pluck out the filling, leaving the wrapper sagging in her bowl. "Some of us care about other things."

"And how are those ambitions going?" her mother retorted.

"Well, actually, I've just started taking classes in psychology! I want to be able to help people."

Bai Run snorted. She did not let Zhao Mei and Wang Lu wash the dishes after dinner; she ushered them out, saying she was happy to clean up but actually was feeling frustrated with her daughter and eager to see them leave.

Several months later, Zhao Mei met her mother to look at apartments in Shunyi.

Their first stop was the Royal Garden complex. Because it was close to a new subway stop, the price per square metre was the highest in the district.

They entered the showroom and stood by a scale model of the complex in giant plastic relief. A salesperson came over with a laser pointer. He had brilliantined hair and was wearing black pants and a white, man-tailored shirt. He looked like he had been polished. He introduced himself as Little Wang and began the pitch.

"To the west is Capital Airport, just a ten-minute drive away, making international travel convenient. To the north, the government plans to build a wetland park covering twelve hectares. To the south—"

"We know the area," Bai Run broke in. "There's no need to explain this. We know exactly what we want: a unit on a high floor, about 120 square metres, with a view."

"We have 180-, 150-, and 90-square-metre units," Little Wang cut in.

"Then 150. Take us to your model unit."

Little Wang led them outside along a wooden walkway atop wet sand, with pools of fetid water on either side, to a building with a completed stone façade. In the hallway, the three selected blue cloth booties from a hamper and pulled them on over their shoes, then took the elevator to the eighth floor. Cleaning ladies sat at the lit entrance to three model units, as potential buyers milled around inside, holding glossy floor plans. The women followed

Little Wang into the apartment.

"We'll have a look on our own," Bai Run told Little Wang. "Does the unit come finished, with the fixtures, or bare?"

The fixtures and appliances, he told them, were just for display, but the development company would provide a designer free of charge to help them choose flooring, overhead lights, cabinets, and countertops, and a colour palette. Zhao Mei paused in the kitchen, admiring the dishwasher – a machine she had never seen in an actual apartment – and the jar of dried corkscrew pasta on the counter next to the imported stove.

"Don't be fooled by those props!" her mother said, coming up behind her. "Pay attention to the workmanship of the basic construction." She pointed to backsplash that had been placed slightly unevenly. "You see?" she whispered. "Shoddy! That is what you need to look for. Suppose we buy it and the pipes leak?"

They learned from Little Wang that high stories cost a little more but could come with a free balcony. They put down 20,000 renminbi on the spot to reserve the right to buy once the development obtained a pre-sales permit. Bai Run called her now ex-husband to tell him the good news.

"I tell you, this area is really going to appreciate in value," she said. "Once the purchase goes through and we move in, we can remarry!" The final purchase and move-in process would take at least three years.

"Glad to hear it," Zhao Gang said.

The spring sandstorms died down and gave way to a sweltering summer. Bai Run still took the bus through

Shunyi every week and got out at the Royal Garden complex to check on construction progress. The hot air shimmered around the high-rises as if they were part mirage. Bai Run would follow the wooden catwalk and think about the trees and shrubs the developer would soon plant on either side. She would imagine looking down from her apartment – she had booked the twenty-third floor – onto a green courtyard with a man-made stream running past a gazebo. She would try to get Zhao Mei to accompany her on these excursions, but Zhao Mei, knowing that her mother would badger the sales staff about completion dates, would decline.

Then one morning Zhao Gang woke up unable to speak or move. His girlfriend, a nice older woman whose existence Bai Run had chosen to ignore, called an ambulance and had him sent to the 301 Hospital, near where they lived. None of the doctors could identify what was wrong with him, and he lay there for three weeks. Bai Run harangued the Party leadership at his institute and got him transferred to the elite wing of a hospital that specialised in paralysis. It was a long way from home, but she planned to stay with Zhao Gang until he was released. She kept the girlfriend out by telling the hospital that she, Bai Run, was Zhao Gang's wife and that only family should be allowed in lest the visits tire him out. So Bai Run made food for herself and porridge for Zhao Gang, then hired a taxi to take her to the hospital, in the Xuanwumen District. She left her BMW at home, as she was worried such an expensive car would be a target for thieves and vandals.

The new hospital, although more comfortable than 301 and its doctors more attentive, had no more ability than the old one to diagnose Zhao Gang. He lingered for a month. In the first week, his colleagues trooped in with special teas and boxes of candy. They would sit next to his bed, hold his withered hand, and talk to him in elevated tones about the latest political education campaign. Soon, they stopped coming, and it was only Bai Run and her daughter, and the occasional relative. These relatives included Bai Run's brother Bai Li, who had taken in Zhao Mei when she was a teenager. He greeted Zhao Gang loudly in English.

"You are going to give him a heart attack with that yelling!" Bai Run said. "As if he weren't sick enough already."

Bai Li had spoken loudly to Zhao Gang on purpose, to flatter him by making sure that others in the hospital heard. Zhao Gang would have wanted everyone in the corridor to know that he spoke English and indeed had spent time as a visiting scholar in America, so Bai Li called out "Hello, Zhao!" He sat by the bed and took Zhao Gang's hand, kneading it in his own and feeling a slight squeeze back.

He turned to his sister, whose anger was rising. "I was just saying hello to him."

"But you're yelling in a hospital," Bai Run said. "You'll startle him to death."

In fact, Zhao Gang never recovered his power of speech, and it was only minutes before he quietly closed his eyes for the last time. Bai Run swivelled to her left, where Bai Li was sitting, and pointed one quavering finger at him, as if barely able to contain her indignation. Bai Run had naturally wavy hair, of which she was proud, and for decades she had enhanced the effect with a perm that tightened it into a helmet of curls. Now, having spent weeks attending to Zhao Gang, wispy tendrils grew out from the curls and were shimmering like seaweed underwater. Her eyes flared wide and red.

"You made such a commotion," she hissed.

"I'm sorry, I certainly didn't mean to hurt him," Bai Li said.

"Well, you did. And me as well. I'm sure you understand that I have a lot to do now to settle his estate."

"You realise you will be disinherited," Bai Li commented with casual covert malice. "You are divorced, and there is nothing to show that he agreed to share the apartment or his bank accounts with you."

A horrified light flared in Bai Run's eyes, but she directed her anger at her brother instead of at herself or her now-deceased ex-husband.

A nurse came in. She felt the dead, desiccated wrist for a pulse then went to find a doctor who would make a formal pronouncement. Orderlies came to wheel the body away. Burial was not permitted in China for ordinary people, and there was just one huge crematorium in the city. They would send Zhao Gang's body there.

"I'll leave you, then," Bai Li said. "I wouldn't want to further upset you."

"And leave me to cope with the funeral arrangements all by myself?"

"I thought you were angry with me."

"That's no excuse for neglecting your responsibility! Old Zhao was your brother-in-law!"

Bai Li stayed behind and paid for Zhao Gang's body to be transported the considerable distance to the crematorium, in Pinguoyuan, on the far west side of the city. There, he purchased a small wreath and reserved a room where the family could gather to read eulogies and bid farewell. He paid 10 renminbi each for ten black armbands and pinned one of them to his sleeve. Bai Li was Bai Run's only ally in the family, and, although he found his sister vexing, he played his role dutifully.

Bai Run wanted an open casket at the memorial. The crematorium did not offer embalming on the safe assumption that no sensible person would pay for it when the body was going to be incinerated in any case. Most people opted for closed caskets. Therefore Zhao Gang's body could not be kept for long before being cremated, and they planned the memorial for the evening of the day he died.

At the service, no one grieved more visibly than Bai Run. She had not allowed the extended family to attend with the excuse that the event had to be planned quickly, so she, her daughter, Bai Li, and Zhao Gang's closest colleague stood before the casket with hands clasped in front of them. Thinking Bai Li's wreath pathetically small, Bai Run purchased a large standing wreath made of paper flowers. She instructed the company that made it to write "For our beloved colleague" on the white sash strung across the wreath's hollow centre. The colleague in attendance wondered who had sent the wreath, but perhaps that was the point. Bai Run wept loudly, her mouth gaping open to show the cathedral of her upper palate. Rivers of mucus streamed down her philtrum, over her lips, and down her chin. She had to lean on her daughter.

Zhao Mei wore black pants, a black T-shirt, and a black jacket over her concave chest. She stood solemnly, head bowed and long, sallow face drawn in grief but without tears. A Chopin funeral march played on the scratchy speakers hanging from the ceiling's corners. It was the signal for the small group to leave.

"What is *wrong* with you?" Bai Run hissed, locking her arm with her daughter's as they walked to the van she had hired to take them home. "Everyone noticed that you have no feeling for your father." Her daughter kept her head bent and offered no visible reaction. "Your father would be so ashamed." Still her daughter said nothing.

They rode home in stony silence. Bai Run had declined to hold a wake or a lunch for the mourners, but she had hung a large photo of her husband on the wall behind a narrow teak table and placed incense, a pyramid of oranges, a small, fat Buddha, and a stack of stale cookies on the table. Now she and Zhao Mei stood in front of the photo, and she instructed her daughter to bow three times to her father. Mother and daughter both bowed, then the daughter flopped down on the nubby couch to watch TV while Bai Run dusted the photo of her dead husband and spoke quietly with him. "Your daughter is here, Zhao, don't you want to say hello? We both miss you. Is it cold where you are? Do you want a sweater?" Then she went into the bedroom and pulled a grey-blue sweater with three buttons at the neck out of a chest of drawers and placed it on the makeshift altar.

After Zhao Gang's death, Bai Run referred to him only in the most reverent terms. He was a brilliant professor whose untimely death took him away from her far too soon. He was a devoted father and husband. He had been handsome and strong, and when he courted her, it was with the delicacy and consideration that only a man of education and refinement could have commanded.

After the funeral, Bai Run occupied herself with plans for the money. She intended to move to the Shunyi apartment, since after all, she was now retired and had no need to remain at the institute, and she spent a week learning about the stock market so that she could invest the remaining cash in high-return securities. She planned to live well off the earnings but even more than that, occupy her days analysing companies.

A month later, Bai Run received notice that pre-sales had opened, and she could make the thirty per cent down payment on the new apartment. They had got the discount price of just 48,000 renminbi per square metre, but the down payment even with that advantageous price would be nearly 1.8 million renminbi, so Bai Run called the bank to instruct them that she would be redeeming the family's investment account.

"I'm sorry, Mrs Bai," the young banker told her, "but the account was redeemed two weeks ago."

Bai Run was outraged. "What kind of theft is this? Who did you let redeem my investment? How could you let this happen?"

"Mrs Bai, the account belongs to your daughter. She inherited it when your husband, sadly, passed away."

"What are you talking about? I am still alive! The wife retains all property until her death! I have been a customer of this bank for a decade! I am going to hang up and dial the police."

"I hope there has been no mistake, Mrs Bai," said the banker. "The Civil Affairs Office forwarded your certificate of divorce. Was that incorrect?"

Bai Run took a minute to respond. When she did, she sputtered. "Yes, that's correct, but it's a fake divorce. We were about to get remarried. Any normal person should know that."

"I do sympathise, Mrs Bai. I have many friends who have done that. But the government does not see it that way. When you are divorced, you no longer have access to your husband's property."

Bai Run slammed down the phone and dialled her daughter. There was no answer. She texted: *RESPOND! YOU HAVE STOLEN MY MONEY! WE ARE GOING TO LOSE THE APARTMENT!*

She waited a couple of minutes and, having received no response, texted: *I WILL NO LONGER RECOGNISE YOU AS MY DAUGHTER IF I DO NOT HEAR FROM YOU IMMEDIATELY.* She decided that a full stop would be more impactful than an exclamation mark.

Zhao Mei texted her back: *Ma, I'm visiting a client. I cannot talk right now.*

Bai Run was sceptical, but she understood there would be nothing gained by saying so. She scrambled two eggs with a tomato, boiled some noodles, and sat eating and brooding. She watched an episode of *The Good Wife* on her computer and headed to bed. She made sure her phone was charged, and the ringer on full volume, but Zhao Mei did not call. By dinner time the next day, she could not stand it anymore.

"Ma," her daughter answered. "What do you want?"

"What do you mean, what do I want? I called the bank to get *my* money, and they said you had taken it! I just have to believe there's a mistake."

"You know the company has not been doing well. We needed that money to make an investment."

Bai Run almost wept. "So it's all true? How could you

betray me like this?"

"Ma, I'm not betraying you. My father left me money, and I'm using it to help my husband's and my business."

"How am I supposed to pay for the apartment that your father and I both agreed to buy?"

"I guess if you don't have the money, you shouldn't buy it."

"So I will lose my deposit!"

"I guess so."

Bai Run was so horrified that it seemed the best response was no response. She knew that Zhao Mei would feel her sense of betrayal over the phone line. There was a full minute of silence.

"Are you still there?"

"I'm still here. I'm stunned to learn I have been betrayed by the daughter I raised and sacrificed for. I should have been more selfish and enjoyed the money I had."

"Ma, you're being dramatic. You have a lovely apartment at the institute, surrounded by neighbours, with a nice garden, and you have a very good pension. You know that I will care for you and make sure you have plenty of money to live on as you get older."

"I don't want to be your charity case," Bai Run nearly shrieked.

Her daughter hung up the phone. She picked up when Bai Run dialled back but said, "It's a terrible signal. I'm in a tunnel. I'll call you back," and she never did.

Bai Run had little choice but to stay home in the apartment at the institute. Each morning, she got up around seven, took a walk to buy a small plastic bag of soy milk and one or two fried bread sticks then returned to eat alone at the small table outside her kitchen. From eight to noon, she watched the news on her laptop and read websites, nervously checking the time as the hour advanced closer to twelve, for Bai Run felt it was uncouth to eat lunch before noon. Sometimes, she started preparing the meal at ten to the hour on the assumption that it would take ten minutes before lunch was ready. After lunch, she might rest for an hour, then she took a walk. A few people might telephone in the late afternoon. In the evening, she watched serial dramas on TV and waited anxiously for 11 p.m., when she could go to bed. Once in a while, a friend would invite her for *mah jiang* and a meal, but Bai Run grew increasingly impatient with these social events. She found that, after the disappointment of her marriage and her daughter, she preferred to be alone.

The new year came around. Zhao Mei and Wang Lu arranged a dinner in a restaurant near the institute and invited Bai Run, Bai Li, and several other family members. They all gathered in a private room around a large table dominated by an immense lazy Susan. Wang Lu had pre-ordered, so food and drink was promptly laid before the seven family members in attendance. Bai Run offered a toast to happier times in the new year, and everyone dug in. There were four cold dishes, eight hot dishes, a soup, soft drinks and beer, and a bottle of wine for toasting.

"To my little sister," said Bai Li, lifting his glass, "who has had a difficult year but manages to look younger and more energetic in spite of it!"

Six of the seven lifted their glasses, but Bai Run was

sitting in the place of honour by the door, arms folded, scowling.

"What's the matter?" her brother asked.

Zhao Mei and Wang Lu also put down their glasses and peered at Bai Run with concern.

"Ma?" said Zhao Mei. Then suddenly, Bai Run burst into tears. She wailed. Her face grew red. Tears spurted straight out from her tightly closed eyes. She heaved and gasped.

"Ma," her daughter said, more gently this time. "What is it?"

"Sister," said Bai Li. "Did we do something to hurt you?"

Bai Run flailed her arms at her brother. "Stay away from me! Haven't you done enough harm?" He stepped back and let his arms drop to his sides.

"None of you really loves me!" Bai Run wailed. "I'm nothing to you but waste, a piece of trash, something you discard."

"Ma," said Zhao Mei, placing a hand on her mother's shoulder, "you know we all love you."

"You!" cried her mother, pivoting and violently shaking her daughter's hand off. "You have no right at all. You are a hypocrite! You sided with him, your father, and you have stolen the money that was to support me in my old age. I want nothing to do with you."

Wang Lu tried to intervene on behalf of his wife. "Please, Ma," he said. "Don't say things you will regret."

"You are no better than she is!" Bai Run told him. "Your wife turned out to be a snake in the grass, and you are too weak to oppose her."

The three cousins in attendance, embarrassed, took

their leave, and Bai Run was left with her brother, her daughter, and her son-in-law. The three stood behind their chairs, staring at her, unsure of what they could say. Bai Run remained seated in the cream-coloured chair with its pleated skirt and large pink-satin bow.

"Let us take you home," said Bai Li gently. "It's been a tiring night."

Bai Run stood and drew herself to her full height. She had stopped crying, and her eyes blazed as if lit with an inner fire.

"Get away from me, all of you. You mean nothing to me. You have all betrayed me, and I will go home and die alone."

Zhao Mei, Wang Lu, and Bai Li all tried to pacify her once again, but each gesture merely added to Bai Run's indignation. Bai Li paid the bill, and the three filed out.

Bai Run sat a while longer clutching her large handbag on her lap. Then, slowly, she rose and walked out of the restaurant. The night was pleasantly cool, and she walked the whole way, about forty minutes, back to her apartment.

F I R E

Phoebe walked through Washington Square pulling her collar around her neck, breathing in the scent of burning wood chips from the townhouses around the square. She felt so much more at home in this strange, exuberant city than back in China, and yet she knew she would have to return. She paused in the centre of the square to watch breakdancers, their teeth flashing and hair blowing back like whitecaps. Turning up Fifth Avenue, Phoebe watched the windows on apartment houses turn gold with the descending sun. When she squinted, the squat buildings looked like sheaves of bound barley; she could almost smell their rich, dusky scent.

Phoebe had grown up in the unprepossessing town

of Changge, in Henan, a flat and dusty place famous for raising hogs. No one in Changge aspired to leave; the chance of success was too remote. The pinnacle of achievement in Changge was to drive a dragonfly tractor, a type of three-wheeler with a long tail that made a loud buzzing noise as it passed. Men hoping to impress would sit atop the driver's seat wearing hats with ear flaps sticking out at right angles, using the long handlebars to steer along the dirt roads.

Residents of Changge were accustomed to the humming of these tractors mingling with the squeals of hogs being trucked into town to be slaughtered. The hogs had a sixth sense about their impending fate, or maybe they could smell the blood of those that had already been killed. Trucks carried ten or twenty live hogs to the slaughterhouse then lined up outside the gates for up to half a day, waiting to sell their cargo, unload, and head out for the next load. Once the truck entered, a beater climbed onto the bed to herd the hogs down a ramp to where a butcher stood wearing a long rubber apron and holding a sharp knife. The butcher attached the pig's hind feet to a chain, pulled the knife across the pig's throat in one long motion, then moved to the next animal as the chain hauled the hog up by its feet to let the blood drain out of its body into a cement tank.

Phoebe knew the pork business intimately, since her father sold slaughterhouse equipment, and she could not get away from Changge quickly enough. A brilliant student, she was accepted at university in the provincial capital, Zhengzhou. She took the TOEFL exam and the GREs and got a scholarship to NYU. Now Phoebe was attending business school there. Although she really wanted nothing more than a job with a decent salary and a nice little house in New Jersey, Phoebe knew that her status in the university rested on being Chinese, and both classmates and professors expected her to return to the mainland to do something impressive. In America, Phoebe would fade into the middle management of a pharmaceutical or chemical company, being hired into the marketing department or that pink ghetto, human resources, while in China, she could become an entrepreneur. She would be invited to dinner with public officials and profiled in magazines, maybe even invited to take a course at the Party School. The problem was, she did not want to go back, at least, not until she met Guowei.

Guowei came to New York as part of a delegation of small businesspeople from Henan Province. Like Phoebe, he came from Changge, where he ran a small sausage company called Changge No. 1 Meat Company. He and Phoebe connected immediately and exchanged small talk about their hometown, like how people ate raw cloves of garlic or the local habit of making a life preserver out of one's pants by tying off the legs and blowing air into the waist. Phoebe took Guowei to all the best Chinese restaurants in New York. He extended his stay, and they became a couple.

Guowei was handsome. He had a long head ending in a square jaw, kind eyes, thick hair, and a pleasing build. He smiled easily. His lean and muscular frame belied a certain gentleness. He had a soft voice and an intent way of focusing on people that women, in particular, found disarming. No one forgot meeting Guowei. Phoebe, on the other hand, was forgettable. She had straight hair that lay flat against her head like a sheet of rain, a snub nose, and chubby cheeks dotted with freckles. She wore two-toned shifts in sensible black and tan or orange squares, and both her purse and her flat shoes would pick up one of the colours of her dress, evoking an elderly person's sense of fashion. She had a certain shyness that people mistook for condescension. But what she lacked in personal attractions, she made up for in business acumen.

For Phoebe, Guowei was a piece of home. She loved his authenticity and openness. She positioned herself as the more savvy partner who would save Guowei from his own trusting nature. They were the perfect complements: where Guowei openly admired others, Phoebe was sceptical. Guowei spoke only Chinese, while Phoebe spoke flawless English. Guowei charmed American bankers, but when it came to funding, they spoke with Phoebe. Phoebe knew all the money men in New York and Sandhill Road, and they trusted her.

Phoebe and Guowei quickly came up with a plan to expand Guowei's business in Changge. Phoebe easily raised a round of capital, and they headed home together to expand the company, which they renamed Airou, or "love of meat". They set up an office in Beijing for Phoebe to supervise, since she had no intention of returning to Henan, and Guowei took charge of the Changge operations.

When Phoebe got pregnant, Guowei was delighted. They got married, since they thought they should. When the baby was born, they bought a separate apartment near their home in Beijing for the girl, whom they named Marian, to stay in with her nanny, and Phoebe stayed nearby so she could visit, initially every day and gradually tapering down to weekly. Guowei spent most of his time at the plant in Changge, but he adored their little girl and often spent his weekends in Beijing, where he and Phoebe would push Marian in her stroller down tree-lined Sanlitun Street and stop to have brunch at one of the cafes. Phoebe disliked Henan and flew down only for the annual sales conference and for Investor Day.

In just under five years, Phoebe and Guowei had become a power couple. They listed the meat company in America with the ticker PIGS. They added to the sausage company an upstream abattoir. It was the first modern slaughterhouse in China, filled with the latest equipment. Instead of small, open-bed trucks, the plant now used three-level closed trucks that carried a hundred hogs. The hogs exited the truck into an anteroom, then a big press pushed them into the slaughter area. There was a tripoint pig-stunning conveyor that clamped around their heads to stun them and dull awareness of impending death. There was a pig hoist and bleeding conveyor, a scalding tank to remove the skin and hair, a skin peeler, splitting saw, synchronised quarantine conveyors for viscera and offal, twin-rail pulleys, and gambrels, all in a spotlessly clean stainless-steel facility that could be observed from behind windows in a viewing gallery. The staff wore bunny suits with rubber boots and paper bonnets.

Investors were ecstatic. PIGS raised more capital, and Guowei negotiated with the city of Shenyang in the north to build a new logistics and distribution centre there. When in Henan, Guowei loved to walk through the slaughterhouse chatting with each staff member and trying his hand at the cutting, washing, and drying machines. Phoebe found the whole business distasteful, but at least this facility did not require that she witness the hogs' distress.

"We have brought the newest and most humane slaughterhouse technology to China," Phoebe said on the investor call. "As you all know, China is a nation of pork lovers. Airou is going to bring the meat industry into the modern age, increasing output and lowering costs. In the last quarter, we doubled our revenue and nearly doubled gross margins. The local and national governments support everything we are doing." The share price soared. Phoebe and Guowei took out loans against their shares and bought an apartment at One Fifth Avenue in Manhattan. They said that Marian would live there when she went to college in the States. If not Columbia, then NYU.

Marian was now a plump toddler of five with mysteriously curly black hair. Her father loved taking her out.

"Can I hold her?" one of the waitresses at their favourite restaurant asked. "I can't believe she's all Chinese. She looks like a mixed-blood child."

"Who knows where she got that curly hair and pale skin," Guowei said approvingly. "Sure, take her. She loves looking at the fish tank." The waitress carried off the squirming child to watch fat carp swimming anxiously in cloudy water.

The couple's life of separation was not without its frustrations for Phoebe. She would meet her female friends over lunch and complain about Guowei.

"He definitely visits prostitutes when he travels," Phoebe told Frances. "I don't care about that, as long as he doesn't bring any diseases home. But he doesn't have the energy for me when he finally appears." She took a long drag on her French cigarette as her friend nodded in sympathy. "I need to have an affair," she concluded. They cycled through men of their acquaintance who might be eligible.

"How about Thomas?" Frances said.

"Too fat. And very full of himself."

"Greg?"

"He talks a good game, but in the end, he would never betray his wife."

They both paused and smoked.

Guowei stayed in Henan the next weekend. "Ten of the hogs they brought in last week were dead. The driver said they died in transit, but who knows? If swine flu turns up in the facility, that's the end of Airou."

Phoebe had to agree. But whether swine flu or some problem with factory equipment, Guowei seemed to return to Beijing less and less frequently.

"Your daughter is going to start school," Phobe said to him on the phone. "Don't you want to be here for that? It's a big company now. The foreman can handle the work you do in Changge."

But Guowei named a series of problems only he could fix. Meanwhile, business was good. Phoebe had an excellent relationship with the analysts covering Airou and spent long hours in phone conversations with them. The company did a follow-on offering. Phoebe and Guowei became wealthy. They put Marian into a Montessori school that cost 286,000 renminbi a year. Phoebe was invited to a course of study at the Party School. She had a brief and discreet affair with a government official of Shunyi District out near the airport, where she and Guowei owned a villa.

Marian loved horses. By the time she was twelve, she had turned into a precocious rider who could jump fearlessly and was already competing nationally. Phoebe and Guowei bought the girl her own horse, which they stabled in Tianjin, and they hired a coach from Argentina. Marian went to live at the Goldin Polo Club during the week so that she could ride every day; she spent her mornings in lessons with a series of tutors to make sure she would not fall behind academically.

Airou's Beijing office occupied the whole twenty-third floor of the China World Summit Tower and now employed eight hundred people. They were selling pork to supermarkets all over the country and selling directly to consumers online. Call bank operators took orders that came in from the internet and dispatched bicycle messengers to deliver to homes. The company maintained warehouses in three hundred cities. Down in Henan, Guowei walked the slaughterhouse floor every day and paused to speak with each employee. In Beijing, Phoebe shut herself in her corner office and took calls from analysts.

Phoebe found herself with more and more time on her hands. She imported a masseur from Thailand and rented him an apartment near her home so that he could be available every evening. She took up yoga. Increasingly, Marian chose to stay in Tianjin over the weekend to get more riding in. She was now travelling within China to national competitions and even occasionally to South Korea and Singapore. She avoided telling her parents about the competitions, since she preferred that they not attend. Phoebe worried about her daughter's estrangement but was in equal measure proud of Marian's riding achievements. She collected Marian's trophies and placed them prominently around the house. She went into the office less and less.

Phoebe's affair with the district official ended without drama. She learned to play golf and spent at least two afternoons a week playing *mah jiang* with three friends. She still met Frances for lunch and cigarettes.

"I work a half day," she boasted to Frances. "Guowei handles the company management. I just deal with the investors and the bankers."

She went to the office in the mornings, arriving around ten and leaving shortly after lunch. Phoebe felt awkward around the staff and tended to avoid speaking with them, preferring to stay in her office with the door shut. One morning, she received a disturbing call from the Airou auditor.

"Ms Wei?" the partner from Ernst and Young said. "I'm afraid we've found a significant discrepancy between your company's statements and its cash accounts, and we will not be able to sign off on the audit."

There was a long silence on the phone while Phoebe absorbed the news. An auditor resignation would drive the stock down at least twenty per cent and might kill the company altogether. There was so much Chinese fraud these days, and undermining investor confidence in the company could spell doom for Airou.

"What discrepancy? I have not been told about this. Our books are clean," she said.

"That may be," said Lawrence, the partner, "but we have not been able to account for nearly twenty million in expenditure."

Phoebe felt ill.

"What do you mean, 'not been able to account for'?"

"The company reported thirty-six million in capital expenditure in the last year on slaughterhouse equipment. We asked for the equipment tax receipts so that we could verify that the money was spent. The accounting department provided receipts for equipment that sells at far lower values. An auditor on our team checked with the vendor. In all, there appears to have been an overstatement of 19,400,017 renminbi."

"That's impossible."

"I'm afraid not."

There was another pause. Lawrence continued. "I'm sorry to tell you that there is more bad news."

Phoebe swallowed and braced herself.

"Your husband has purchased an apartment for exactly the amount of the overstatement."

"Purchased an apartment where?"

"Here in Beijing. Sanlitun."

"That's impossible. He is never in Beijing, and when he does come, we have a home out in Shunyi, at the Riviera."

Lawrence paused. "Have you not seen the *Beijing Evening News*, then?"

Phoebe felt ill, again. "I don't often read that paper. Why?"

"They have a photo of your husband in Beijing," Lawrence said, "in a somewhat compromising position with another man."

Phoebe felt she might throw up. She stepped outside to smoke, then she dialled Guowei's number.

"The auditors tell me you bought an apartment in Sanlitun."

"I did."

"And you didn't think to discuss it with me?"

Guowei did not answer.

Phoebe continued. "You just took the money from the company?"

"Phoebe," he said. "I started this company long before you appeared. I am there every day solving problems and driving the business forward. You sit in Beijing having lunch with your friends. I only took what is already mine."

"To take what is yours you have to embezzle?" She had walked out on the terrace.

"That's insulting."

"The equipment receipts were all inflated."

"I don't know anything about that. I just asked accounting to free up the cash for me."

"Guowei, do you understand that you have destroyed this company? How could you do this to us? What is the apartment for anyway? Who is supposed to use it? If you don't want to live with me, there are more straightforward ways to say that." But as she spoke, the reality of the situation dawned on Phoebe, and she wondered why she had not seen it before.

"Have you been together a long time?"

"What do you mean?" asked Guowei. "Been together with whom?"

"Come on. The *Beijing Evening News* thought it was newsworthy enough to have a photographer wait for you and that man. I hear it is not just a friendship."

"I don't know what you mean," said Guowei. "I was drunk, and a friend was helping me back to the apartment."

Phoebe put down the phone. She went downstairs to the newsstand in the lobby and bought a copy of the

Beijing Evening News. In the photo, Guowei had his arm draped around the neck of an angular young man and was whispering something into his ear.

Phoebe took the elevator down to the garage, where her driver was playing cards. He jumped up when he saw her. She told the driver she was going to Tianjin to see her daughter. They set out immediately. Along the way, the car passed clusters of empty towers, high-rises where there had once been farming villages. She looked at the vast cement expanses, the vertical cranes standing idle on the sites, the construction hoists and rod climbers, and for the first time, instead of hope and progress, she saw waste and desolation.

It took about two hours to get to the Goldin Polo Club where Marian was staying. When they drove in, Phoebe saw that Marian was riding Lucia, a racing mare, on the main track with her trainer. Phoebe addressed him in English.

"I need to borrow Marian. Can you take Lucia back and rub her down?"

Marian cantered over. "Ma, what are you doing here? I'm practising. I have a competition on Tuesday."

Phoebe wanted to make sure Marian never saw the photo in the *Beijing Evening News* or the other articles that were bound to come out about her father's gay lover.

"I've found you a boarding programme in America," Phoebe lied, "and you need to start immediately or they won't hold the place." Marian was shocked and unhappy, but she was also accustomed to her mother's caprices. With some difficulty, Phoebe got Marian packed up and into the car. On the way to Beijing, she emailed the principal of a Chinese boarding school in Nyack, New York, and wired a semester of tuition fees from her bank account. By the time they arrived in Beijing, the school had agreed to send a car for Marian to Liberty Airport in Newark, and Phoebe had bought her a ticket on United Business Class for the next day.

With Marian disposed of, Phoebe was free to stalk the Sanlitun apartment. Guowei had said he was staying in Henan for the weekend. On Friday, Phoebe had a late dinner then waited across the street from Guowei's apartment building. She stood in the shadows under the willow trees that lined the street, smoking. The moon was out, and Beijing's sky was unusually clear. She stood and watched for an hour, maybe two, thinking back to her first meeting with Guowei in New York, when they had talked long into the night. She thought, this is why he turned the warm beam of his attention so intently onto me: it was strictly intellectual. Guowei's charm came from his disinterest. He could focus attention and inquire deeply because he had nothing at stake. Phoebe had felt seen and understood, but it turned out that was precisely because Guowei did not particularly care.

It was a warm summer evening, and stragglers spilled out of bars, leaning on each other's shoulders and laughing. The air grew chilly, and Phoebe zipped up her thin hoodie. It was after midnight. She stood diagonally to Guowei's building so that she could see the doorman, who was behind parked cars. At 1 a.m., she was about to give up, when a taxi drove into the semi-circular driveway of the apartment building and stopped in front of the lit entrance. A doorman leapt forward to open the rear passenger door, as someone in the cab leaned over the front seat to hand money to the driver. In a moment, long legs stretched out of the open door and planted feet on the pavement. A man ducked his head and unfolded so that he stood straight. He was tall and angular, with shoulders like a clothes hanger, wearing a white scarf with a velvet jacket. He reached into the cab and extended a hand to Guowei. It was the man in the newspaper. They went through the doors that were being held open for them, walking a zig-zag path that betrayed their drunkenness, down the brightly lit hallway to the bank of lifts, where the friend pressed a button and they both went upstairs.

Phoebe hailed a cab and went home to the Riviera.

The next day, she purchased a plastic canister and got her driver to find a station and fill it with gasoline. She went to four newsstands and bought all their copies of the *Beijing Evening News*, until she had a stack as tall as herself. She waited until the early hours of Sunday morning then drove herself downtown in the Mini they kept for personal use, with the canister of gasoline in the rear compartment.

She entered Guowei's building by simply waving to the doorman then, instead of stopping at the lifts, walked to the back and propped open the stairwell and the fire exit. In the deserted alley at the back of the building, she took newspapers from the tightly bound stack, soaked them with gasoline and stuffed them between bushes and the building. Once she had built a reef of gas-drenched newsprint, she twisted one newspaper into a makeshift torch, lit it with her cigarette lighter, and set the end alight.

Flames seemed to sprint from back to front, until a half corona of orange fire surrounded the steel-and-glass foundation. Phoebe saw with satisfaction that the open fire door had sucked flames into the building and presumably up the stairwell.

For a few days the fire at Sanlitun was the biggest story in the country. Twenty-three people died. Guowei and his friend escaped, but with disfiguring burns. Marian rushed back from America, and she and her mother visited Guowei at the Burn Unit of Anzhen Hospital, where they wept, fed him orangeade through a straw, and demanded the best possible doctors. Airou's share price could not recover from the scandal, but Phoebe managed to raise the capital to take the company private again. When Guowei was discharged, Phoebe initiated divorce proceedings.

WANT WANT

A perfect little boy took a sugared rice cracker from his grandmother's hand and bit into it with his small white teeth. Bai Song and his wife, the grandparents, rapturously inclined towards him with expressions of anticipation melting into bliss. It was a Want Want cracker, but also much more: a symbol of family unity, of love, of desire, of gratification, all expressed in one bite. Cut. They did sixteen takes. The cellophane packets drifted to the floor. Off camera, the boy grimaced at the taste. But they got it just right.

Anyone who watched television would know Bai Song and Li Li as the kindly grandparents in commercials for rice crackers, insurance, instant noodles, and vitamin drinks. The first thing travellers arriving at the Beijing airport would see was the elderly couple smiling over the luggage carousel as they sat with a Bank of China representative comparing investment products. No family on the west side of Beijing was more perfect, Bai Song so tall and grave, his wife so effervescent. The gentle crinkles around the eyes, the abundant white hair, the still-elegant frames dressed in their familiar cardigans – they seemed to express virtuous lives well lived.

But their neighbours noticed things television viewers did not. Like the family's disappointments – the iterative failure of Bai Song's get-rich-quick schemes, the older son's history of truancy, an odd effeminacy in the younger son that no one dared label. But they took an indulgent view; the parents, after all, were icons of Chinese social harmony.

The neighbours' indulgence evaporated when Hao Weijun returned from his multiyear stay in Nairobi, and everyone saw that the Bai boys, who had never resembled their father, were not, after all, the mysteries of nature that everyone had assumed. In fact, both of them looked just like Hao Weijun.

"You're fatter" was all Xiao Liu, Hao Weijun's wife, said when she met Hao at the airport. He had expected more enthusiasm after those years of separation, but then, he and Liu had never really got along that well.

"We've all got older," he responded. Xiao Liu had let her hair go grey in the nineteen years of his absence. She wore a form-fitting woollen jacket and stretch pants whose rounded surfaces betrayed thick long johns worn underneath, a depressing touch for her husband, who had spent two decades living in the warmth of East Africa without snow or biting winter winds. Xiao Liu's ankle-high boots were topped with artificial fur. Compared with her fuller, rosy form two decades earlier, she was shrunken, wizened, not at all like the rounder figures of Kenyan women that Hao Weijun had got used to. And her perm made her hair seem as if it had been placed on top of her head, like a helmet.

Xiao Liu pushed ahead through the crowd as Hao Weijun followed with his cart piled high with zippered bags.

"Slow down, what's the rush?" he said.

"It's a long way to the parking lot," she responded crisply. "Beijing isn't the backwater you left twenty years ago. You could probably fit ten of the airports in Kenya into this one building."

Hao Weijun said nothing but picked up his pace. They pushed through the long tunnel to the parking lot, and Hao Weijun waited while his wife brought the car around.

"When did you get a car?" he asked.

She clucked her tongue. "Perhaps you think we're magically rich. I borrowed it from the Bai family. Their younger son has done very well as a tour guide."

Hao Weijun said nothing, recognising a treacherous topic. He loaded the suitcases into the trunk of the Audi, and they drove to the compound where they lived, on the west side, near Hangtian Bridge. Little had changed in nearly two decades, except that, instead of bicycles, small cars were parked in the dust outside the individual entrances to the low rises.

"You see?" Xiao Liu said. "China has developed a lot in all these years. You probably don't even recognise it."

Hao Weijun, again, said nothing. He got out and

opened the trunk to unload the bags.

Bai Song had been walking a small white dog on a path through the bushes across from the low-rise complex. He saw the arrival and hurried over.

"Hao! You're back from Africa!" Bai Song gripped Hao Weijun's arm and shook vigorously with his left as they clasped right hands. Bai Song had always treated him as a brother, in a sort of backhanded defiance of the general view that Hao was unnaturally close to his wife.

"You've gotten grey," Hao Weijun said to Bai Song by way of greeting. None of them mentioned Bai Song's wife or his boys.

"That grey hair is famous in television commercials all over China now," said Xiao Liu acerbically to her husband. "If you'd come back for holidays, you'd have known that. The Bais are famous in China now. But I know you didn't have anything so advanced as television down there." Hao ignored the comment.

"It's true, I've got a lot older," Bai Song said.

"You look great," said Hao Weijun, clapping him on the shoulder. "Thanks for lending the car. It's nice not to have to wait in a taxi line."

"It's Bin's car," Bai Song said, referring to his younger son. "He's doing very well. I'm sure you remember him and his brother, Bo?"

Hao Weijun had never understood whether raising the topic of the boys was Bai Song's way of challenging him or whether he had buried the truth somewhere deep inside his psyche.

Hao Weijun bent down to pat the dog. "You'll have to excuse me. I'm really tired from the flight. I need to grab something to eat and have a nap."

46

"We all know how famous your Liu's cooking is," Bai Song commented jovially. "I'm sure you'll be happy to have some real Chinese food again."

Xiao Liu had already stamped up to their fifth-floor apartment, leaving her husband to carry the bags. It took him three trips. When he lugged in the last, large bag, he opened it and carefully took out a carved ivory elephant wrapped in tissue paper. He stretched out his arm to his wife, but Xiao Liu, now sitting on the couch and watching television, without turning her head gestured for him to leave it on the cushion next to her.

"Is there anything to eat?" he said.

"You can heat up the noodles if you're hungry."

Hao Weijun put a pot of noodles on the burner then ate alone in the kitchen. When he was done, he stripped down, showered, and collapsed on their double bed, sleeping until the early hours of the next morning. Xiao Liu, he found, had slept on the couch.

Bai Song returned to the two conjoined apartments he and his wife shared on the first floor of the unit two doors down from Hao Weijun and Xiao Liu.

"Old Hao is back from Africa," he called out. His wife was washing dishes in the small kitchen.

"Really? I wonder how that will go over with Xiao Liu." Bai Song's wife never hesitated to raise the topics that others left buried.

"I'm sure it will take a short period of adjustment, and then they will be very happy together," said Bai Song, the pacifier.

Hao Weijun had not been back from Kenya in nearly

twenty years. The official story was that he had been working on the railway that China was building there and preferred to send money to his wife rather than take the biennial home leave that the production brigade allowed.

But it was whispered that Hao Weijun had an African wife and several children in Kenya. Someone who lived at the Hangtian Bridge apartments worked in the Swahili Section of the radio station downtown and had heard this rumour from a consular officer in the embassy in Nairobi. Someone else heard that construction of the railway had ended five years before. Everyone speculated about whether Hao Weijun would return to his wife in China. But then they heard from a neighbour's niece that Hao Weijun's state-owned employer, generally forbearing about long-term absences, had issued an ultimatum to him: come back to Beijing or give up retirement benefits. Hao Weijun had duly returned.

After Hao Weijun had slept, he drank some coffee with milk, waited for the light, then took a stroll around the complex. Outside, he saw Bai Song's wife for the first time.

"You want to take a walk? We could go to Purple Bamboo Park," he proposed.

"Hao! I'm happy you're back," Li Li said brightly. "Let's just sit here on the bench and catch up."

"I missed you," he said, looking directly into her eyes.

"Well, we all missed you!" Li Li was still using the tone of a Want Want spokeswoman, managing to project her voice while also sounding warm. "I'm sure Xiao Liu will be wanting to spend time with you. There is so much to catch up on!"

"She doesn't seem to be too interested in my life."

"Give it time." Li Li placed a hand on Hao's thigh and squeezed slightly. Hao Weijun's heart sped up. "It's been nearly two decades, with nothing but phone calls! Just see, after a couple of weeks, the two of you will feel like newlyweds again."

"How are the boys?" he said with a little more wistfulness than was, perhaps, appropriate.

"My pride and joy! Bin is a tour guide. He has such an outgoing personality. I think that's why he earns so many tips. That's how he bought the car. An Audi!"

"And Bo?"

"Still looking for the right job and the right girl. So nice of you to ask after them!" Li Li's expression was a mask. She might have been talking to the grocer. She gave Hao Weijun a bright smile. "I need to start lunch. The boys are coming over. Come by any time! Bai Song would love to sit down with you and hear all about Africa. You know how he's always talking about starting a business. You two might just find that Kenya will be your pot of gold."

"I think if I were going to get rich there, I'd have done that long ago." But Li Li was already taking her leave.

Now that Hao Weijun was back, the neighbours all noticed his bulging eyes that squinted half shut, his un-Chinese curly hair, his tanned skin, curiously similar to the Bai boys'. They remembered the close friendship between Hao Weijun and Li Li. At a time when it was unusual for unmarried men and women to spend time together, Li Li and Hao Weijun took private walks in the park and went skating together. Neighbours remembered that Hao Weijun had been sent on a delegation to Tanzania and had come back with a pair of denim bellbottoms for Li Li. Neighbours raised their eyebrows, but they saw that he also brought a carton of cigarettes and a shortwave radio for other friends, so perhaps he was just accommodating people who wanted imported goods.

For Hao Weijun's first month back, Bai Song's friendliness with him kept gossip at bay. Bai Song went to Purple Bamboo Park each morning with Hao Weijun to perform Tai Chi. They went fishing together one weekend. They sat together on the stoop in the courtyard in fine weather smoking and talking about soccer. The wives were cool to one another, but those two had very different personalities.

The Bai boys themselves started to notice their resemblance to Hao Weijun.

"Isn't it funny?" Bai Bo said to his mother one afternoon as they sat together eating hotpot. "Everyone is saying how much Bin and I look like Old Hao, as if maybe he were a long-lost uncle."

Li Li had insisted that her sons come to lunch on Sundays, and she made a special effort to feed them well. Today she had mixed up bowls of sesame sauce into which they could dip the thin slices of mutton that they had cooked by dunking them in the boiling water of the hotpot. There were platters of sliced lotus, cabbage, mushrooms and three types of meat.

"Don't be ridiculous," she snapped. "What could Hao possibly have to do with our family?"

"He kind of looks African himself," said Bai Bin. "Maybe living there for a long time starts to make your hair curly."

"Then what happened to you?" his brother asked.

"As if you were any better! You look like you walked out of the jungle in New Guinea."

"Just eat your meal," Bai Song said. "Your mother spent all morning preparing this for you. It's better than a restaurant!"

All eyes turned back to their bowls. When they were done eating, the Bai boys cleared up, then the four of them watched a variety show on television. The portion devoted to showcasing performers featured a famous female army singer named Song Zuying.

"Everybody says she has a child with President Jiang," Bai Bin announced. Bai Bin had studied Cantonese and was a tour guide for groups from Hong Kong. They all knew the latest gossip about stars from the Hong Kong media.

"Nonsense," said his father. "I am surprised that you listen to garbage like that, an intelligent boy like yourself." Bai Bin was twenty-five. "He would never have got to be president if he carried on with other women. The Party does not allow behaviour like that."

Bai Bin rolled his eyes at his brother but said nothing.

They said goodbye around eight o'clock. Bai Bin drove his brother home in the Audi.

"I guess we both got the ugly genes," he said, as they pulled out of the compound.

"Maybe it's the nutrition Mom got when she was pregnant with us," Bai Bo said. "Those were tough times. They didn't have enough to eat. Maybe that made our skin dark."

"Must have been something like that," said Bai Bin.

Bai Song and Li Li sat in the half-darkness watching television after their sons had left. The small dog, Doudou, sat on Bai Song's lap.

"Don't forget we need to be at the studio at seven tomorrow morning," he said to his wife.

"I haven't forgotten. What is it, insurance?"

"Yes, Ping An. That little boy will be in the shoot."

"Little monster."

Bai Song had loved Li Li from the first moment he saw her, in a production of *The White-Haired Girl* at her factory. Bai Song had just left active service in the Navy and was assigned to an engineering institute in Beijing. He was already thirty, and his family and friends felt that the time for marrying was well past. A Navy friend brought him to the performance in the eyeglass factory, in which Li Li was playing one of the friends of the heroine, Xie'er, who came to her aid in the very first scene. When Li Li took the stage, presenting the heroine with paper-cut pictures for the new year, she turned to face the audience with a defiant look. The red make-up around her eyes accentuated the sense of a burning stare. Bai Song was captivated.

Bai Song had always been an obedient boy, deputised by his parents to make sure his younger siblings did as they were told. He adopted that familiar role, of helpmeet, in his marriage, doing all the housework and the cooking and accompanying his wife most Sundays for a meal at her parents' home rather than joining his siblings in visiting his own mother. Bai Song was unfailing in his devotion to his wife and seemed to have forgotten his own family. In the lean years, he and Li Li had double rations of meat and even got milk for the boys because of

Bai Song's Navy affiliation, but they never shared with his brothers' and sisters' families. Yet when Li Li's father got Alzheimer's, Bai Song invited the old man to live with them, giving him the best bedroom, while he and his wife moved into the small room that the boys had shared when they lived at home. He fed his father-in-law gruel in the morning and pushed his wheelchair for an hour-long daily promenade in fine weather. Bai Song bathed and toileted the old man with tender care.

Bai Song had made several forays into business to earn some more money. Each autumn, everyone in his research institute was issued sets of 366 calendar pages – one for each day of the year plus a cover sheet – and asked to assemble and staple them. Workers were paid a piece rate for finished calendars. Bai Song would set himself higher and higher targets, bringing home the stacks of calendar pages and setting his whole family to work all night long for three or four days in succession. One year, he had tried to sell catalytic converters on behalf of a factory headed by an old Navy buddy, but he had failed to capture the attention of automotive companies that might purchase the converter and then eventually dropped the idea. He still had a box of the ceramic honeycombs at the back of his closet.

Many times, Li Li urged Bai Song to go in with Hao Weijun, who had a better business sense, on a trading company. Hao Weijun had been exporting small battery-powered devices, like flashlights and mechanical toys, to East African buyers who paid in peanut oil, which fetched a high price on the Chinese market. Hao Weijun was building a nice nest egg for his family.

Bai Song saw that Hao Weijun had good business

sense and consulted with him. Bai Song was determined to buy his wife a fully automatic washing machine, which was very expensive. He was determined that his wife would be the first in their complex to own one of these luxuries. But to buy one, he would need to bring in extra money.

Hao Weijun had got mood rings from an acquaintance who worked at a jewellery factory. They had large, cat's-eye stones in open bands that could be squeezed to fit any finger size and that were made of eighteen-karat gold. Hao agreed to give Bai Song three hundred of the rings on consignment. The acquaintance wanted eighty yuan for each ring, so if Bai Song could sell them for 300 yuan each, the two could split the difference.

Bai Song thanked Hao Weijun and took the case of rings downtown to the "free market" near the American Embassy that foreigners called Silk Alley. He had obtained an introduction to one of the stall owners.

"Brother," he said when he got there, opening the jewellery case with its royal-blue velveteen lining. "I managed to get these rings at a very good price. I think foreigners will snap them up. If you help me sell them, I'll give you everything I make over 300 yuan per ring."

The stall owner, a large northerner with heavy-lidded eyes, picked up one of the rings between a thumb and fat forefinger, wrinkling his nose as he eyed the object, as if he had caught an earthworm.

"No one is going to pay 300 yuan for this," he declared. "The band is open. Foreigners like a closed band, and they are the only people who would pay money for these."

Bai Song suspected that the stall owner was trying to talk down his price. "Tell you what: I'll stay with you and make the pitch. I speak some English." Bai Song thought that if he left the rings, the stall owner might sell them at nine hundred or a thousand and pay only three hundred to Bai Song. Businesspeople, he knew, could not be trusted.

"Come in the evening. Saturday afternoon is very busy, and I won't have time to show you the ropes."

Bai Song agreed and cycled home, returning that evening at seven.

"You want to start with a price that's at least double what you're willing to settle for," the stall owner told him. "When people pass by, say something personal. 'Sir', 'Lady', 'Young Man', anything so that they know you are speaking specifically to them. A lot of people will get irritated and will be rude to you. That's okay. If you get one person in twenty to stop and look at the rings, that's good. Then one in ten of those will make a purchase."

Bai Song made notes in a small notebook he'd brought along. He looked up from the notebook. "I'm ready, Brother!"

Bai Song stood outside the stall hailing all passers-by. "Look at the mood rings! These beautiful stones change colour with your mood! Set in the purest gold!" Several people stopped and looked over the tray of rings. A couple even tried them on. One offered twenty yuan for a ring. He made no sales and stayed until eleven, when almost no customers were left.

"You can come tomorrow if you want," the stall owner said, apparently pitying Bai Song. "I know it's hard for an intellectual like yourself to sell at an outdoor stall, but it gets easier. Sunday afternoons are really busy."

"Don't worry about me!" said Bai Song. "I'll get the hang of it." He closed the case of rings, fastened it to the rack of his bicycle, and pedalled home.

The ride took an hour, and he was famished when he got home. Li Li had left a bowl of rice and a dish of cabbage stir-fried with dried shrimps. As he ate, she came into the kitchen in the Mickey Mouse T-shirt she usually wore to bed. She stroked his hair.

"How did the sales go, my brave entrepreneur?"

"Not bad. Mr Wang is showing me the ropes. Tomorrow I'll make a lot of sales."

"That's great. Eat up and get some sleep. Tomorrow will be a big day."

Bai Song turned up at nine the next morning and had to wait an hour for the stall owner to come open up. From ten until eight in the evening, Bai Song called to customers, demonstrated how the rings changed colour, and moved his starting price from eight hundred to two hundred. In the end, he sold two for seventy each and rejected several offers to buy at thirty and below. As the big northerner packed up the stall, Bai Song could not hide his dejection.

"I'm afraid the rings are just not popular right now," the stall owner said to him. "If you could get something with Disney characters, I'm sure I could find customers for you."

Bai Song thanked him and returned the rings to Hao Weijun. He gave Hao Weijun all the money he had earned.

"You are so thin-skinned!" Li Li told her husband. "You were not aggressive enough. Why should you be embarrassed to earn a living like any honest person? Honestly, your family has such airs." Bai Song had to accept that he was not cut out for business, and he could not give his wife all she wanted and deserved. When the boys grew up, they bought their mother an automatic washing machine.

The Sunday evening after Hao Weijun had returned, Li Li and Bai Song went to bed early, tired out by their sons' visit. They lay for a short time in the dark in the twin beds pushed close, with only a narrow space in between. Bai Song was lying on his side facing away from his wife. Li Li wasn't sure if he was awake.

"I wish Bo would find a girlfriend," Li Li said. "It's high time for him to marry."

Bai Song was quiet for a while, then he spoke. "Li, do you think they know?"

"What are you talking about?"

"You know. About Hao being their dad."

"Don't be ridiculous."

"They look like him."

"Let them. You have dark-skinned relatives. And we didn't have much nutrition in those days. Their growth could have been stunted."

"I guess so."

"I know so. Relax. Remember, we agreed it was for the best."

"If I'd been able to have children, you wouldn't have had to do that."

"That again! Can you stop?"

Bai Song turned out the light. Li Li rolled over to face the other direction, so that their backs were to each other.

"Good night. Don't think so much."

Bai Song did not respond. He stared at the wallpaper until he could make out the purple tracings in the dark, then he closed his eyes and fell asleep.

HELLO, KITTY

Bai Song told everybody about the Japanese toilet that could sense when you were coming into the bathroom and raise its lid automatically, as if it were greeting you. The new apartment also had a garbage disposal, something that no Beijinger had ever seen before. A compactor made it easy to dispose of trash. There was a dishwasher, a clothes washer, and a dryer, even though most Chinese thought dryers ruined clothing. The refrigerator had a screen you could write your shopping list on and that reflected the temperature inside the machine and in the room and could tell you when you ran out of eggs. The floors were heated from underneath so you could go barefoot in winter if you cared to. All these amazing conveniences had come with the apartment, not like those cement boxes most developers were selling.

Bai Song's younger son Bai Bin had found the place for his parents and taken charge of selling their large but simple ground-floor apartment in Hangtianqiao. In addition to the modern conveniences, the couple got a lot more space in Mentougou. The building even had an underground parking garage. The only negative was that Bai Song and his wife would have to wait for the district to fill up. Technically part of Beijing, Mentougou lay on the other side of a serpentine road that wound through forbidding mountains. It served as the second line of defence between the Great Wall protecting China from northern barbarians and the precious beating heart of the emperor inside the Forbidden City. People hushed as they drove into Mentougou, with its the sudden light and cold shadows, as if they were entering a cathedral. Even inside Bai Song's high-rise, there was a smell of dripping water, as in a cave.

Bai Song and his wife were retired, he from an engineering institute and she from a factory that made polarised progressive lenses for eyeglasses. Bai Bin had persuaded them that comfort was what they wanted in their old age – floors that would be heated in winter, garbage you could send down a chute. They were, after all, growing frail. There was plenty of room in the new apartment for their sons and for Bai Bin's daughter – both boys' wives were estranged – and Bin and Bo kept their belongings in Mentougou but seldom visited, as it was inconvenient. But sometimes the old couple missed being in the complex where they had lived for forty years. They talked about the friends they had left behind in Hangtianqiao.

"I wonder what's happening with Hao and Liu," Li Li would remark to her husband about a couple who had been their neighbours for decades. "All those years when he was in Africa, she acted like she was mad that he didn't come home, but I think she got used to being independent. Now she's got to live with him."

Bai Song remembered the early years before Hao Weijun left for Kenya, when the two would bring their birds to Purple Bamboo Park together, hang the cages in the trees, and do *qigong* breathing exercises, seldom exchanging words. Li Li had more complicated memories of Hao but kept them to herself.

"I hear he had a hip replacement," Bai Song commented. "She'll have to help him around the house. She never reckoned on having to take care of him in his old age." Bai Song and Li Li were privately gleeful that old age and its infirmities had descended on their friends at Hangtianqiao; it made living out in this distant suburb seem like the smart choice.

"Shall we go outside?" Li Li suggested. "It's sunny, and there's no wind."

Locking the security gate over their front door, they stamped their feet in the deserted hall to wake up the sensor that would turn on an overhead light, then they waited for the elevator to come to the twenty-third floor. If anyone else had moved into their tower, they had not yet met. On the first floor, they checked the dusty mailbox, which was empty except for a flyer wedged into a crevice outside, then they stepped out into the broader world, squinting. Slowly, holding each other's arms, they made their way along a flagstone path to the garden in the middle of the complex, with its crabbed forsythia bushes and pavilion on a small hill. Management had apparently thought better of the planned lily pond, because it had been dug but there was no water.

"It will be lovely when this place fills up," Bai Song remarked.

"I like it deserted like this," said Li Li. "Imagine if there were six or seven times as many people." A shadow passed across the pale disc of the spring sun, and the old couple grew cold.

"Enough for today?" said Li Li. They took the elevator back upstairs, relieved, and poured water from the thermos into a pot to make tea.

The complex in Mentougou started to fill up, but not exactly as Bai Song and Li Li had anticipated. One morning, Li Li took the elevator to the ground floor to go to the little shop that sold daily necessities – milk, rice, green onions, toilet paper, a few dusty bunches of carrots – to residents who did not want to trek to the hypermarket in town. There were usually a couple of elderly neighbours sitting on small stools outside the shop playing cards or chatting; there was not much for a retiree to do in the area. Today a gaggle of young people, at least eight of them, stood around the entrance. Most were smoking, though they could not have been more than fourteen years old. They looked to Li Li like a flock of exotic birds, some with spiky hair dyed scarlet or white or blue, some wearing heavy make-up, all wearing clothes made of denim and leather with silver studs running up and down the legs and around the waist.

"Excuse me, can I get through?" Li Li said to a girl who had a thick stud in her lower lip and whose hair was dyed blue. The girl turned to look at Li Li straight on with dead eyes that showed white underneath the dark, inscrutable pupils. "That's a very interesting hair colour," said Li Li, looking for something to say. The girl glared at Li Li for a moment then slowly stepped aside. She threw down her cigarette then walked over to a white moped that was parked on a strip of mud outside the store, stepped over the seat, pulled a pair of sunglasses from the top of her head over her eyes, put her feet on the pedals, and rode away.

Li Li leaned over the counter in the dark store to speak quietly with the proprietor, a heavy, amiable man who just two years before had farmed barley on the site of the high-rises.

"Where do these kids come from?" she said in a low voice.

"It's a bunch of teenagers from Cuandixia Village," the proprietor whispered. "The government moved them here to fill up the junior high. It was embarrassing to have a new high school and no students."

The district government had built a "magnet" high school with a brick façade and turrets. Long, blue-green lawns had to be re-sodded every six months but looked very impressive. The school could accommodate five thousand students. The district had already hired teachers and administrators, mostly farmers who had been displaced by the development, but they needed at least a few dozen students before they could open.

"These children have to travel back to Cuandixia every evening?" said Li Li. "That doesn't sound practical."

"No, the government moved them into some of the empty units here at the complex. They can go home on weekends."

Li Li bought some salt and cooking oil and headed back upstairs.

The next afternoon, she and Bai Song were returning from a dancing class at the Cultural Palace in the village as the sun began going down. When they reached their floor, they saw that the door to the apartment across the hall was ajar.

"Maybe a family is moving in," Bai Song said. "Shall we introduce ourselves?"

They put their things down inside their own apartment then stepped across the hall and tapped on the door, pushing it open. Four teenage boys were sitting in the gloaming around a camp stove with a can of paraffin burning white and blue in its metal stand. All four looked up simultaneously. To Li Li they looked like wild children, heavily ornamented, with dyed hair and clothing that was too tight. The girl from the store strode in. Li Li saw that she was wearing an expensive-looking leather jacket, short-waisted, with a lot of complicated straps.

"Somebody ask their grandparents over for a visit?" she said to the group.

"We live across the hall," said Li Li. "We saw your door was open and wanted to welcome you to the building."

Two of the four boys went back to scrolling through something on their phones. The other two continued to gape at Bai Song and Li Li. The girl was clearly in charge.

"Where are your parents?" asked Bai Song. "We'd like to introduce ourselves."

The girl snorted.

"It's just us, old man," one of the boys called from the middle of the room. He was girlishly thin and had long, feathered hair that interfered with his eyes. The girl called him Xiao Liu.

"Well," Bai Song said, unsure of how to conclude the conversation. "Let us know if you need anything." He and his wife left the dark apartment and headed back to their own place.

"Hold on," said the girl, following them. This appeared to be the signal for the four boys to stand and troop after her. "We don't have any gas. It makes cooking kind of tough. We eat a lot of instant noodles."

"That's terrible," said Li Li. "Would you like to use our stove?"

Bai Song scowled at her and shook his head, but it was too late.

"Absolutely." She turned to the others to issue orders. "Pangzi! Get the wok! Xiao Liu, rice!" The two went scurrying into the apartment and came back with the wok and a small bag of rice. The five entered Bai Song and Li Li's apartment.

"Wow, this is way better than our place," said the heavyset boy she had called Pangzi.

"What's your name?" Li Li asked the girl.

"You can call me Kitty. Like Hello Kitty."

"Well, Kitty, go right ahead and use the stove."

"We don't have any cooking oil."

Li Li took out the large plastic container of cooking oil she had bought just yesterday. Kitty poured a generous helping into the wok and turned on the flame. She turned to Li Li and Bai Song, who were watching.

"We don't have any meat either."

There was an awkward silence before Bai Song spoke up.

"I'm afraid we can't help you with that. Is there

something you can substitute?"

But two of the boys were already rifling through Bai Song and Li Li's refrigerator.

"Excuse me!" said Li Li. "If you need something, we'll get it for you. Please don't go through our refrigerator." The boys ignored her, and when Bai Song started towards them, the boy with the feathered hair shoved him back so that he fell into a chair. Kitty whipped around.

"You old people had best just stay where you are. You're pretty frail, and we wouldn't want you to get hurt."

Li Li looked at her husband in a panic. Her breath came quickly.

"Now see here!" she said to Kitty, more loudly than she'd planned. "The five of you are being very ill-mannered. I am planning to go see your parents and tell them about these goings-on."

Kitty turned to look at her. "Nie," she said, and the one with dark skin and an angular face, like a jackknife, walked over briskly. He slapped Li Li hard across the face. Li Li was so stunned that she did not notice the pain. She placed her right hand on her cheek as if to make sure it was still there. Bai Song tried to stand to go to her, but Pangzi, standing in front of him, pushed him back. A fourth boy, who had bad acne and hair that tufted up like a duck's, leaned back in his chair and smirked.

"Now you old people just calm down," Kitty said. "We're going to cook ourselves a proper meal." She instructed two of the boys to tie the old couple to their chairs. They used jackets from the closet, tying the arms around the backs of the chairs, while they looked for something more appropriate. Nie found two rolls of packing tape in a kitchen drawer. The four boys wound the tape around and around the two old people until they looked like moths in cocoons.

Next the teenagers dug into Bai Song and Li Li's refrigerator and took out jumbo shrimp, leeks, pork, eggs, mushrooms, and various sauces that Bai Song had prepared, and they cooked a big meal, which they ate with gusto without offering any to their hosts.

"Can we have something to drink?" Bai Song said.

"Nie, give them some water," said Kitty. Nie filled a glass with water from the faucet embedded in the refrigerator and held it to Bai Song's then Li Li's lips while they drank, spilling considerable amounts on the front of their clothes.

"Now look what you've done," Kitty chided. She tossed two hand towels to Nie, who put one each on Bai Song's and Li Li's shirts.

Xiao Liu found a case of beer in the pantry off the side of the kitchen and broke it open, handing the beers around.

"None for you, old man," he said to Bai Song. "You old people have to be careful of your health."

"There's got to be money in here," Kitty said. "Let's look." The five teenagers found Bai Song and Li Li's stash, which held about 10,000 renminbi. They divided it up then trooped around the apartment trying all the appliances while Bai Song and Li Li remained tied. Pangzi seemed particularly fascinated by the toilet.

"Kitty! Hey look! You can heat the seat and spritz yourself with water as you sit here and poop." He took down his pants and sat to demonstrate. "This is so awesome."

"Pangzi!" called Xiao Liu from the laundry room.

"Got any clothes to wash? We can do it really fast here."

"Let's wash our quilt!" Kitty said. "It's filthy."

Nie was sent to fetch the quilt. They stuffed it into the front-loading washer, added at least two cups of washing powder, then pressed the buttons at random until the machine started up. All five of them peered through the little window.

"What a great apartment," said Pangzi. "Hey, we could take the refrigerator to our place. Then we'd have plenty of space to put food."

When the food was done, Kitty and the four boys squatted on the kitchen floor each holding a bowl of rice and eating the shrimp and pork dishes. When they finished, they left the bowls streaked with tomato sauce on the round Formica table. Chopsticks glistening with oil lay across the bowls.

"Can you at least let me get up to go to the bathroom?" Bai Song asked. "I can't hold it this long. And I'm worried about my wife sitting in one position for all this time."

Kitty surveyed Bai Song and his wife. Li Li's calves had gone white with the pressure from the tape.

"Nah, you can just go where you are," she said to Bai Song. "Guys, let's get that refrigerator moved."

The four boys unplugged the large, double-door refrigerator and together pushed it out of the apartment and across the hall. Presently, they returned and sat on the kitchen chairs to smoke. A dark square was left in the linoleum where the refrigerator had been.

"Maybe we should just move in here," said Nie.

"What are you saying? These nice old people already live here," said Kitty. "We'd have to get rid of them, and we don't want to do that."

Xiao Liu snickered. "With your dad being chief of police, I don't think we have to worry about consequences," said Nie.

There was a dripping sound. Li Li looked over and saw that her husband had wet himself.

"Will you look at this old man?" said Kitty. "That's just disgusting."

The boy with acne held his nose theatrically. "Eww! These old people really don't have a lot of self-control, do they?"

Kitty was looking up at the ceiling. After many trips to home decoration stores, Li Li had chosen a chandelier with crystal that dropped from the brass brackets like tears and that held twenty bulbs that worked off a dimming switch. The chandelier cast shards of coloured light across the walls, as its hanging bulbs swayed and the crystal drops tinkled. The chandelier made Li Li happy every time she turned it on.

"Nie, Xiao Liu: get some tools. Let's take that chandelier," Kitty ordered.

"Please," said Li Li. "We can give you money. If you'll just let us call our son, he can get a lot of money for you. Don't tear our apartment apart."

Kitty just laughed, and the boys imitated her. Just like jackals, thought Li Li.

Presently, Nie and Liu came back from their apartment with a screwdriver.

"Pull over a chair. Nie, you spot him," Kitty instructed.

Xiao Liu stood on the chair on his tiptoes as Nie held up his hands to break a potential fall. Xiao Liu unscrewed the eight screws holding the brackets in place, and Nie and Pangzi took the heavy light fixture from his hands and carried it into the apartment across the hall. The five then walked around the apartment looking in drawers and in closets for any valuables they might have missed. Although unsure whether Bai Song's watch and Li Li's jewellery were worth anything, they took both in case. Kitty found a box containing Bai Song's diaries. She stamped out her cigarette on the wooden floor then opened one of the notebooks at random and read out loud:

"There are those who say actresses are unreliable," Bai Song had written, "but I know in my heart that Li Li loves me and will always be faithful." Kitty hooted with laughter.

"So cute, the way these old people talk about love." She looked up at Bai Song. "Did you also worship Mao Zedong? Did you want to give your life to the revolution?"

Bai Song did not respond. Nie went over to his chair and hit him across the face with the back of his hand.

"She's speaking to you!"

Li Li gasped. Bai Song's lip was bleeding. His eyes watered.

"I did admire Chairman Mao," he said, "until he started instigating violence. When the Red Guards stormed into people's houses and beat people up, I could not support that."

"You're lying, old man," said Kitty. She flipped to another page in the diary and stood to read with a mock salute. "Today we went to Tiananmen, where the Chairman himself greeted us. May he live for ten thousand years!"

The teenagers all stood and broke into a raucous rendition of the national anthem.

"Stand! People who refuse to be slaves!" they sang.

"What about you two?" said Kitty, addressing the old

people, still tied to their chairs with packing tape. "What kind of Chinese people are you, not standing for the national anthem?"

"You may have forgotten that you tied us down," said Bai Song. Nie, who was playing with a baseball bat he had found in the closet, suddenly swung with all his might at Bai's right arm, taped to the chair. There was a horrible cracking sound. Bai Song yelped once but then steadied himself and glared at Nie. "If this is what you want to do," he said, "go ahead."

"Hey, Kitty," Xiao Liu said softly. He directed Kitty's attention to Li Li. She was slumped in the chair, eyes closed, mouth agape and leaking saliva.

"What's the matter with her?"

Kitty looked her up and down.

"Probably some old person thing, like a stroke. Look, let's get out of here. Cut them loose," she said. The boy with acne and the stout one, Pangzi, took turns with a box cutter slicing through the tape. Li Li slumped to the floor. When he was released, Bai Song sprang to her side. His pants had a dark stain in the middle.

He knelt by her chair. His right arm hung uselessly. He held a cup of water in his left and tried to get his wife to drink. "You'll be okay. Just drink some water for me."

The five teenagers had left. Bai Song got up and closed and locked the front door. As he did, the power went out. His wife whimpered.

"I'm glad you're awake. It's just another power cut. There's no need to worry; those kids are gone."

He used his left hand to fish his phone out of his right pocket. He flipped it open and pointed the screen light at the floor to illuminate a path to the living room. He helped

71

Li Li to stand and walked her over to the couch, where she lay down. Bai Song sat in the chair opposite. The floor under his feet was toasty warm.

LOVING YAN HONG

Beijing's seasons are like a siege: spring, with its screaming sandstorms; thunderstorms every summer afternoon; an autumn so dry it feels like the sky is cracking open; and winters so cold you wonder if survival is guaranteed. In the brief seasonal interludes, the city goes calm, like a sailing ship in the doldrums. It was on such a still autumn day that Bai Jie stood outside an apartment block by the west Third Ring Road, pulling up his jacket collar and watching a lighted window where the family of his nephew Bo was eating dinner.

He had been there for nearly two hours, watchful, waiting, hoping that Bo's housemaid, Yan Hong, would pass by the window. Just a silhouette or a glimpse of the geometric black-and-yellow stripes on the sweater she perpetually wore over her blue pants, that would be enough to make Bai Jie's breath catch and his eyes close momentarily. Without her, Beijing was incoherent, with its cement towers flung along grim avenues. But when Yan Hong passed across the lighted window, the city gathered around her into a whole.

Bai Jie had never expected to become interested in a girl; it had been decades since he had even noticed a woman. Before retiring a decade earlier, at sixty, he had been a truck driver, which in his prime was a highly coveted job. Truck drivers could travel to other provinces and obtain unusual foods or scarce goods. He had once brought a burlap bag filled with shelled peanuts back with him from Shanxi Province. Another time, he had bought grapes in Gansu and then driven back as fast as possible so they would not spoil. His wife and daughter proclaimed them sweet.

Bai Jie dressed like a huntsman, in a vest of uncombed sheep's wool that hung in long strands from his torso, making him look at once bigger and rougher. His face was lined and wind-weathered, his frame tall and rangy. As a teenager, Bai Jie had been in a reform school and had killed a man.

Bai Jie's wife was college-educated and had been beautiful, with full breasts, a heavy shock of black hair, and transparent skin. But her family were reactionaries; she was considered lucky to have made a match with Bai Jie, a son of the working class. "Don't worry about anything," he told her as they sat together in the park. "I won't let anyone bully you." And she believed him. But as with so many unions of that era, the balance of power shifted over the years, until no one remembered why Wang Dong had married the coarse, hard-drinking Bai Jie.

When he had visited his nephew's apartment one night a year earlier, he had been expecting just a cup of tea and a chat to break up the long trip home. Bo's place was near where Bai Jie had to change buses. When Yan Hong brought him tea, their eyes met, and Bai Jie saw that she was looking at him with coquettish amusement, unmistakably treating him as a man, not as Bo's aged uncle.

Yan Hong was seventeen, fresh from a rural village in Hebei Province, thin and coltish. When she spoke to Bai Jie, she looked straight at him instead of looking down demurely. Bai Jie experienced a stirring that he told himself was protectiveness towards a country girl who had never before lived in a big city. On impulse, Bai Jie proposed to his nephew that he and Bo could share the cost of Yan Hong. He would take her home to take care of his wife, who was recovering from hip surgery. Bai would pay her, but she could spend two days a week at the nephew's apartment, cleaning, doing laundry, and shopping. In this manner, the nephew could save money without admitting that he had over-extended himself. The deal was arranged.

After Yan Hong moved into Bai Jie's apartment, Bai Jie felt a vague but unmistakable lifting of the spirits. He got up earlier than usual and often whistled or sang, wondering whether Yan Hong thought he had a nice voice. He chose pieces of Peking opera that flattered his reedy tenor. He took special care with his pigeons, which he kept in a large coop on the roof, speaking tenderly to them as he watered and fed them, making sure their anklets had not chafed, setting two or three free to fly across the rooftops and back, so that they could exercise their wings. Then he took his songbirds for a walk, shrouding their wooden cages and swinging a cage from each hand to simulate branches swaying in a storm, so that the birds would have to cling to the perches and strengthen their legs. When he removed the shroud, the birds would sing for an hour.

Throughout these ministrations to his menagerie, Bai Jie ignored Yan Hong, who was busy heating soy milk and fried bread for their breakfast. But he was aware of her presence as of a source of heat, and when she went out, the temperature in the room dropped ever so slightly.

Bai Jie started spending more time in the apartment, at least on the days when Yan Hong was there. When she went to his nephew's, Bai Jie would bicycle over in the evening to escort her home. They said little on these brief trips. When he arrived, he would simply nod at her and say, "Ready?" and the ride home up Baishiqiao Lu was quiet except for the swish of their tyres. When they arrived, they dismounted and pulled the ring locks closed inside the spokes of their rear wheels then climbed the five flights of stairs to the apartment, where Yan Hong started dinner. This silence was the most companionable in Bai Jie's memory.

Over the new year, Bai Jie asked Yan Hong to call her parents to wish them a happy new year. When they answered, he took the phone.

"Sister and Brother," he said with exaggerated courtesy. "I swear to you your daughter will be safe and happy in our home. I am grateful that you entrusted her to us." His eyes welled up with tears, and he put an arm around his wife's shoulders. "My wife feels as I do.

Yan Hong is like a daughter to us."

Bai Jie thought he started to notice signs of interest from Yan Hong. But then he would curse himself for his vanity, because how could a teenage girl, with so much confidence and good looks, possibly be interested in a gaunt old man like himself?

"Why is that girl asking you to speak to her parents?" his wife said to him one evening. "What have they got to do with you? She's a queer type."

"No idea," he said, studying the newspaper, but his heart throbbed in his chest.

"You know, birds are just like mammals," his friend Wang Shi remarked to him as they walked in the park one morning, swinging their shrouded bird cages. "When they're courting, the female scopes out the male's territory and learns about his preferred companions and places. It's just the same with apes."

"How do you know?" Bai Jie said.

"I read it in an American magazine. It's very authoritative."

"What do the males do?"

"They bring food to the females."

Bai Jie said nothing more, but he stopped at the corner store on the way home and bought two boxes of soft yellow cakes with cream in the middle. He gave one to his wife.

"Why'd you buy that?" she said.

"I know you like sweets."

She looked puzzled but took the box and put it on top of the small refrigerator.

He waited until the afternoon, when Wang Dong had gone out walking, to give the other box to Yan Hong. She immediately opened it up, tore open one of the six cellophane packets, and bit into the cake. She looked up at him as she consumed the sweet. Bai Jie had planned to act nonchalant about the cakes, saying he had bought an extra box by mistake, but he blushed deep red and stammered, "It's just something I picked up."

He thought he noticed Yan Hong looking at him, then he told himself he was allowing his hope to distort his judgement. But then one morning, her interest became unmistakable. The two were alone in the apartment, Wang Dong having gone shopping to find a dress she could wear to the flamenco class she had signed up for. Bai Jie was standing on a chair in the main room of the apartment, taking down the curtains that stretched across the glass door to the balcony to fix a broken joint between two rods. Yan Hong saw him teeter and brace himself against the wall, and she hurried over and put her hands on Bai Jie's hips to steady him.

"You have to be careful, Uncle," she said. "If you fall at your age, it will be serious. Why don't you let me do that?"

Sheepishly, he got down, but in doing so, he took the hand she offered him, and it was as if he had put a finger into an electric socket. A dizzying pulse ran through him; he could not think clearly. Yan Hong looked up at him and held his eyes. She reached up and kissed him on the lips and he kissed back. Then he pulled away.

"I'm so sorry," he said. "Something came over me. I apologise. Please, let's pretend that did not happen." But Yan Hong had not let go of his hand. He drew her more tightly to him. He was overwhelmed; he wanted to cry.

When Wang Dong came back in the evening, she noticed the box of cakes stacked up on Yan Hong's pile of belongings. She checked to make sure that the other box was as she had left it, on top of the refrigerator.

"Did you give Yan Hong a box of cakes?" she asked her husband.

"I bought two by mistake. I didn't want to go back to the store to return the second one."

Wang Dong said nothing more.

Bai Jie and Yan Hong began a sexual relationship. Wang Dong adopted an attitude of studious ignorance. She went out in the mornings, because she found distasteful the spectacle of this mooning seventeen- and seventy-year-old. Her pride dictated that she should give them every opportunity. She was not particularly angry and certainly not jealous. That would have been ridiculous.

Bai Jie's daughter, however, was less forgiving. Bai Hua visited unannounced one morning to give her mother a sweater she had knitted. She entered the apartment with her key and walked straight into the day room, where Bai Jie and Yan Hong were lying together on the sofa bed. Yan Hong was wearing a slippery lavender camisole. Bai Hua's father wore only a Smurfs T-shirt. They yanked the quilt over them to cover their lower parts, but there was no mistaking what had been going on. Bai Hua quickly closed the door and stammered, "I was just leaving this sweater for Ma. I'll leave it here on the fridge. I'll be going now."

"Hua, hold on," her father said, pulling on the long underwear and blue jeans that he had left crumpled on the floor. He pushed his feet into a pair of flimsy white slippers from the Hotel Otani and opened the door. "I was having a nap. Yan Hong was just helping me."

"Helping you do what?" Bai Hua said with a sharp

note of sarcasm.

"I've been ill," he attempted, desperately. "She wanted to take my temperature. Please don't leave."

By this time, Yan Hong had pulled on her clothes and shuffled out of the room, keeping her eyes to the floor, to boil water for tea.

Bai Jie pleaded with his daughter. "I think you are imagining things, Huahua," he said, using a childhood nickname for her. "Can we please forget this?"

"You mean not mention it to my mother?" Bai Hua looked at her father, and he averted his eyes.

Once Bai Hua had found them out, her mother could no longer pretend to be ignorant. It was decided that Yan Hong should move back to the nephew's apartment and Wang Dong should hire a new housekeeper. She selected an older woman from Gansu, weathered, stringy, and devoutly Buddhist.

The forced separation from Yan Hong was what occasioned Bai Jie's vigil outside his nephew's apartment building. He stood, eyes fixed on the lighted window five stories up. When a figure crossed in front of the window, Bai Jie's heart leapt.

Bai Jie continued the daily watch for two weeks. Then he could bear it no longer. He went to his nephew's apartment and knocked on the door.

"Uncle!" his nephew said. "Join us. We were just sitting down to dinner." He pulled up an extra stool to the round table, which was laid with a pork, egg, and tree fungus dish; green beans stir fried with garlic; a tomato-egg soup; and white rice in a green enamel pot. His nephew filled Bai Jie's rice bowl and gave him a pair of chopsticks. But Bai Jie did not eat. He just stared at Yan Hong, who was carrying the dishes in and out of the kitchen, replenishing rice in bowls, locating soup spoons. Wordless, Bai Jie fixed a mournful gaze upon her. His deep-brown eyes clouded over with a milky film of emotion. His nephew wondered if the old man had developed cataracts.

"Are you all right, Uncle?" said Bo.

Bai Jie did not respond. Yan Hong, clearing dishes, looked across the table and returned a gaze equally sorrowful. Shocked, Bo understood what he saw. But his uncle did not care.

That evening, Bai Jie returned home and fired the woman from Gansu. He told his wife that Yan Hong was coming back. Bai Hua visited and pleaded with him to be reasonable and spare her mother's feelings, but Bai Jie would not be swayed. At seventy, he had not expected much more from life, but now there was Yan Hong. She had inspired him with so much tenderness that it leaked out like a light from under a thin blanket. Bai Jie had come alive for the first time in decades, and he would not relinquish that.

Freed to spend their days together, Bai Jie and Yan Hong slipped into a routine of housework, walks, and caring for the animals. They spoke together in almost a private patois. Walking or cooking or feeding the pigeons together, they moved in coordination, as if unconsciously following a choreography. Wang Dong, feeling she had no role, spent more time at her adult classes and at the pool, where she swam three times a week.

In a way, it was emancipating for her. She had been grateful to Bai Jie when he married her. Back then, she was shunned by friends and neighbours, who would walk by without acknowledging her. She had to sit through nightly criticism/self-criticism sessions in which even the woman next door, whom everyone despised for being demanding and arrogant, lectured her about her backwards political ways, and Wang Dong could only nod and say, "Thank you, Sister." Bai Jie rescued her from all that. They had Bai Hua, who absorbed all Wang Dong's time and love for a decade, and Bai Jie was always away on his long hauls to the western provinces.

In the end, though, they did not have much in common. Wang Dong had a wide range of interests. She had learned ballroom dancing and was starting to do oil painting. She loved to travel. She had a bridge group. Bai Jie, by contrast, had got old before he was fifty. The Ministry of Materials had folded, and Bai Jie's position was eliminated. He was allowed to choose between operating the elevator in their building and taking early retirement, and he chose the latter lest his neighbours make fun of him, sitting all day on a stool in the elevator. From that point on, Bai Jie stayed at home, watched television, cared for his menageries, and took long naps. Wang Dong could not even get him to walk with her in the park.

Her husband's relationship with Yan Hong was embarrassing, but Wang Dong reasoned that few people would believe they were really having an affair – it was so unlikely. She and Bai Jie were grandparents. The time for affairs was well past.

After Yan Hong had been back at Weigongcun for about three months, she announced to Bai Jie and Wang Dong that she had to go home to Hebei for a week to get married. Her parents had made arrangements for her to marry a neighbour with whom she was acquainted from school. She showed them a picture: the man had a long, lined face and big ears, as if he needed to dispel heat.

Bai Jie took her to the train station in the back of a tricycle truck and anxiously saw her off. He bought a ticket for the platform and stood there a long time looking after the train. "You are coming back?" he had asked just before she boarded. "Of course," she responded, but he did not feel completely confident.

Just two days later, Yan Hong texted him a photo of herself with her groom. He, wearing a white Western suit with blue piping around the lapels, was jokily on one knee, with hands up in imprecation. Yan Hong, wearing a powder-blue dress with puffy sleeves (Bai Jie had never seen her in anything but pants), was pretending to be stand-offish, head turned away from her suitor and a hand up warding him off. Bai Jie chuckled. The joke picture covertly expressed her loyalty.

While she was gone, Bai Jie tried his hand at poetry. "Your face, like the moon, lights my night. Your eyes, like the stars, fix my position." He tore it up and threw it in the waste basket. He texted her, *We're getting along fine. Don't hurry back. Congratulations!* then waited anxiously for her to text back. After an hour, during which he grew nearly despondent, she texted him a smile emoji, and he was reassured.

Yan Hong returned in a week wearing a simple gold band and showed Bai and his wife pictures of her and her new husband, holding hands in front of a seascape, leaping into the air in front of the Eiffel Tower, kissing, with a big red heart behind their heads. Bai and Wang both commented that the photography shop was very skilled.

Bai Jie began to treat Yan Hong differently. He would not let her do any lifting. He made breakfast in the morning and let her sleep in. When Yan Hong began vomiting in the morning, Wang Dong understood.

"Was your marriage night that successful?" she asked. "Should I congratulate you?"

"It's true, and the baby is making me so sick, I'm sure it's a boy," Yan Hong said.

"You'll have to go home and let your husband take care of you."

"He's working in Shanghai. He cannot afford to quit his job. Neither can I."

"But what will you do?"

Yan Hong looked pleadingly at the older woman. "If you will allow it, Auntie, I will stay here with you and Uncle. It will be good for my baby to live in Beijing."

The realisation struck Wang Dong suddenly and unpleasantly. Yan Hong was never going home.

"Of course, you are welcome in our home." What else could she say? Her husband had desperately wanted a son.

In the spring, Yan Hong went home to Hebei Province to have her baby. Bai Jie went along on the excuse of expressing proprietary concern; his age was excellent camouflage. The new husband duly appeared at the hospital but spent his time scrolling through news feeds and messages on his phone. He was in a long-term relationship with the wife of his construction team's boss in Shanghai. Marriage was a convenience for him and also a way to carry on his bloodline without a lot of effort. He had no thought of caring for Yan Hong or making a life with her.

After the birth, Yan Hong stayed four days in the hospital with seven other women on the maternity ward, with a white curtain to separate her bed from the others when she needed privacy. Bai Jie and Yan Hong decided to call the boy Yu for "universe", and of course he had to have his father's surname, Liu, so he was Liu Yu. Bai Jie kept a vigil outside the observation room, where the babies were kept in cribs with plastic covers, and when the little boy woke, Bai Jie followed the nurse as she brought the baby to Yan Hong to be breast fed.

"Brother and Sister," Bai Jie said to Yan Hong's parents, who had come to the hospital to bring boiled eggs and sweetened date soup to the nursing mother. "I cannot bear to see your daughter separated from her child. My wife and I would like little Liu Yu to come live with us in Beijing." The family could hardly object, since Liu Yu would have access to much better schools and better medical care in Beijing than in his mother's rural community in Hebei. So it was that Bai Jie's illegitimate son joined the household.

Yan Hong continued to cook for the family and to handle the housework. But she and Liu Yu moved into the small bedroom that had belonged to Bai Hua years earlier. Clearly, sleeping in her old place outside the kitchen would be too disruptive now that a child was involved. But the private room elevated her status. Although she was still a teenager, young enough to be Bai Hua's daughter, the unacknowledged position of her son as Bai Jie's own gave her a special place. Wang Dong was irritated, but she was still the wife. She told Bai Jie that she wanted them to renew their vows. They bought a white suit for Bai Jie, a plum-coloured dress and a straw hat for Wang Dong, and went to a studio to sit for a whole album of photos in which they held hands and looked longingly into each other's eyes. They invited a few friends for a big dinner, and they sang karaoke. Wang Dong felt she had made her point.

At home, while Bai Jie continued to dote on Yan Hong, she grew distant. It did not matter to him. Bai Jie was fascinated by the boy and indulgent as he had never been even with his granddaughter. Every morning, he waited for Liu Yu to wake and sometimes crept into the little room to watch him sleeping next to his mother. He stared at the round, reddened cheeks and the tonsure of black hair and thought about how *boyish* Liu Yu looked, as if he might jump out of bed at any minute ready to play. When Liu Yu did finally get up, Bai Jie was waiting for him at the door to take him up to the pigeon coop on the roof. Liu Yu wrapped his hand around Bai Jie's forefinger, and they took the elevator to the top floor then mounted thirteen more steps to the roof, where Bai Jie imparted the mysteries of raising birds. Little Liu Yu called him "grandfather" and liked to be carried, which Bai Jie would readily do, delivering him to his mother when they got back to the apartment as a priest might hand custody over scripture to a novice.

In the early years, Yan Hong would bring her son back to Hebei every year for the extended new year holiday, and the child would see the man he called father. After three or four years had passed, Yan Hong's husband disappeared from the conversation. At first, she would go home to spend the holidays with her parents, but by the time Liu Yu was six, she gave up going to Hebei.

Liu Yu grew into a wiry, thoughtless adolescent, preoccupied with his friends and heedless of his family. He had big ears like Bai Jie but otherwise resembled his mother, with a small round nose, freckles, and tiny, bright eyes, like an animal's. He conducted himself with a careless cruelty, and since his mother and Bai Jie both doted on him, they shrugged it off as humour.

"Why haven't you left me any dinner?" he would yell at his mother, coming in well after the family had finished eating.

"I thought you would eat out with your friends," Yan Hong would say. "Just give me a minute." Liu Yu was the only person to whom she would defer. She spooned some rice out of the pressure cooker then took a plate of eggplant out of the refrigerator.

"It won't take me a minute to heat up."

"That slop?" Liu Yu said, looking at the plate of eggplant with exaggerated disgust. "Never mind. I'll make instant noodles."

"There's no nourishment in that," his mother said. "They give you stomach cancer."

"Cancer would be better than eating the shit you make."

Yan Hong gave up and put the eggplant back in the refrigerator.

The boy grew up in the Bai household, but he did not have a Beijing residence permit and could not attend public school there, so Bai Jie used the money he had made from selling his deceased mother's apartment to send the boy to an expensive private school far out in the Beijing suburbs. The proprietors were willing to overlook the boy's lack of papers in return for a comfortable fee. Little Liu Yu lived at school during the week and, increasingly, stayed over on the weekends as well. The trip downtown took at least two hours each way.

When he visited home on the weekends, Liu Yu spent

most of his time playing games on his phone. He seemed to have a whole private life contained in the phone. Bai Jie would cook his favourite dish, salt-and-pepper shrimp, and would not let anyone else eat the shrimp. The boy could eat fifteen or twenty at a sitting.

After lunch, Liu Yu would ask Bai Jie for money, tell his mother not to wait for him to come back for dinner, and head out with a mysterious gaggle of friends. When he came in, he often seemed to have been drinking. Liu Yu was impatient with sitting in classes and did poorly in school. Bai Jie, now in his mid-eighties, on the final Saturday of every month would take three buses out to the school to see him.

On this particular Saturday, Bai Jie set out at seven, bought a box of oranges for the boy, and took the long bus ride. He arrived around ten, laboured up the path, greeted the guard at the gate, and asked the woman at the desk in the lobby of the dormitory to inform Liu Yu that he was here.

"I'm afraid Liu Yu is not in. He got a pass to go to town this morning. We don't expect him before dinner."

"Ah. Well, I suppose I'll wait." Bai Jie sat down on the couch across from the reception desk. The woman at the desk brought him a cup of tea. Bai Jie had a look around the lobby, so much fancier than the environment he had grown up in. Fat goldfish with long ears swam behind a small castle sitting on the bottom of a tank behind the receptionist. There were long fluorescent lights in the ceiling and a grey, low-pile rug laid down in squares. Bai Jie napped on the modular couch. It was after five before the boy returned.

"Grandfather! What are you doing here?"

"I told you I was coming."

"You meant *today*?" Liu Yu said. "I thought you were talking about tomorrow!" The exaggeration in his voice made it clear that Liu Yu was mocking the old man. "You must have been sitting here waiting!"

Bai Jie gave his son the box of oranges he'd brought.

"Grandfather, you should know I can't eat all these. What did they cost? About eighty yuan? Take them back and give me the money instead."

"I don't know why you always need money. What do you find to spend it on out here?" But Bai Jie peeled off eight tens and handed them to Liu Yu.

"Grandfather, you should know that young people these days need money. Everyone else in my class has money. Their parents give them allowances every month."

"Shall we have dinner?"

They went to the special refectory where students could eat with guests. The food was expensive, but there wasn't much choice, since the school was so remote. At six-thirty, Bai Jie got up to leave. The last bus was at seven.

"Liu Yu, I'm leaving."

The boy looked around at the old man. "Yeah? Okay, have a good trip. You don't need me to see you out, do you?"

Bai Jie shook his head and started down the path to the bus stop, carrying the crate of oranges.

As he reached his late eighties, Bai Jie's heart condition made him increasingly unable to walk more than a few paces without stopping to catch his breath. He went less often to see Liu Yu at school, and soon the boy graduated and went off to a technical school in Jiangsu Province to study hotel management. He returned to Beijing at the new year for a long holiday, but he spent the whole time out with his friends. Soon, he had a girlfriend whom he'd bring to the apartment. Without introducing her to Bei Jie or his mother, Liu Yu would take her into the little bedroom, now his alone, and shut the door.

Yan Hong and Bai Jie had given up any pretence of being employer and employee; she now slept in the big bed with him. Since Liu Yu was mostly gone, Wang Dong took over the bedroom. They said nothing about this new arrangement and continued to cook and eat together companionably enough. Wang Dong told the neighbours that Bai Jie's health was failing, and they needed the girl to help out, which was true enough.

Bai Jie saw less and less of Liu Yu. He knew the boy did not care for him. It did not matter. Liu Yu came back at holidays, and Bai Jie would insist on doing the cooking himself. He could no longer bend down, so after washing the rice bowls, he left them out on the counter. He enjoyed being busy in the kitchen, where he could muse about his son's future. It was just like being in love.

MCKINLEY AND THE CAPTAIN

McKinley had come to China eighteen years earlier, wife and infant daughters in tow, with a plan, though he could not have articulated it. Once both daughters had left for college, he and his wife realised they were tired of each other, and Marianne had moved back to Michigan. But McKinley did not let go of the apartment in Beijing and kept extending his company contract, six months, then a year, as if unsure whether he would really leave. Living in Beijing demanded an explanation, and McKinley did not have one yet. Instead, he lingered.

McKinley was all the firm wanted in a "China hand", a partner they regularly brought in front of clients to suggest the boundless promise of the market. He possessed a piercing light in the eyes, like a great actor who creates a centre of energy on stage even when others have the lines. He communicated restlessness without moving. He tapped fingers lightly on surfaces he passed, and he walked leading with the ball of his foot, luxuriating, as if enjoying the feel of moss underfoot. He was ravenous for sensation; his wolf's eyes rummaged in corners of rooms for anything unusual. His greatest enjoyment came when people in his landscape caught his eye momentarily, recognising that their privacy had been invaded but that he would keep their secrets. Sometimes he deepened his voyeur's pleasure with a slight raising of the eyebrows; confederacy. When he entered a room, everyone in it became a potential collaborator; it was bracing.

Now that his family was gone, McKinley eschewed the claustrophobic life of international schools, foreign housing compounds, embassy receptions, and press club events and began living like a local, or so he thought. He imagined that the Chinese executives he had met through the firm would provide him with a key to authenticity and perhaps even meaning.

He had taken to visiting the Ghost Market on Saturday mornings with Captain Wei, an associate of the firm. McKinley tried to interest Captain Wei in typically Chinese artefacts: a stone carving of a lion for the garden; a Republic-era teapot; someone else's posed family photos from the 1940s; but the captain inevitably dawdled over items he found more modern, like an oil seascape or a garden gnome. He chose a rhinestone bracelet and matching necklace for his daughter, buying them from an old man who had laid a tablecloth out on the paving stones of the market. He was selling jewellery from Walmart in Arkansas, where he had spent three months caring for a new grandchild.

Captain Wei, in McKinley's estimation, by virtue of his position as an executive of the China Ocean Shipping Co, held a key to the mysterious clockwork of the Chinese economy, a mechanism that, if only opened, might answer a question as yet unspoken about a generation that had surrendered its agency to a greater good, about violence and redemption. McKinley believed, without articulating the thought, that if he were inducted into Captain Wei's private world, he would understand why he had come to China.

Captain Wei had a small, curved frame with bow legs and a doorknob head with a comb-over. He dressed in Western suits with a tie and matching pocket square. He spoke carefully, knitting together his sentences with the most elevated vocabulary, and he had strong opinions, mostly positive, about China's best-known poets and philosophers. His imagination inclined him not towards art, however, but to industry, the factories that were the great productive engines of daily life, from which ribboned out unbroken streams of shoes, paper, clothing, coal, appliances, furniture, bricks, tiles, toys – all the props of modern life. To Captain Wei, "businessmen" were artists of the material world, a bold and able race who could burrow into the arteries of social life and create value from mere clay. The irony of McKinley and Captain Wei's Saturday morning excursions was that neither man liked the other.

"You must come to dinner with my family," Captain Wei said to McKinley on one of these weekend excursions.

"That would be lovely," McKinley said.

"Monday?"

McKinley could not think of a reason to decline, though he was depressed at the prospect of a cab ride to the west of the city and hours of making small talk with Captain Wei's family. On Monday evening, he duly purchased a sack of oranges and hailed a cab to Yuetan, the "temple of the moon" street on the west side of the city, where Captain Wei's family lived in a company-issued apartment. He mounted five flights of stairs. A dry bunch of leeks leaned against the door frame, and a diamond-shaped red poster pinned just below the peephole showed the character for "wealth" upside down – a Chinese pun for wealth arriving. McKinley rang the bell and was ushered in. There were Captain Wei, a birdlike woman who was his wife, and their daughter, who called herself Swallow in English.

Wei's title, "captain," was a bureaucratic rank rather than an honour earned at sea. He had spent his life in charge of cargo inspections, and the special fees he received from foreign shipping companies had enabled him to buy a house in America for his retirement. Port inspections, after all, could be fast or slow, and when a ship full of fresh tuna was threatened with two weeks' demurrage, the cargo owners would do pretty much anything to persuade the captain to expedite the process of unloading cargo. Captain Wei had a sizeable chunk of cash waiting for him offshore for when he finally decided to leave China. He fully intended to enjoy many years of leisure in New Jersey before he died, but before moving to the house he had purchased, Captain Wei needed to find a suitable occupation in America for his daughter. The easiest path was to create a job for her at a business that he, Captain Wei, would establish.

And he was fully ready: he just needed the right opening. Captain Wei felt he had not yet taken advantage of the new wave of capitalist entrepreneurialism washing over China. He went to bed each night dreaming of schemes that would make him truly rich. The friendship with McKinley was a step in the right direction. As a partner in a large consultancy, McKinley was privy to the secrets of many foreign companies; he could offer Captain Wei privileged access to the richest lanes of commerce.

Swallow was all that her parents were not: tall and stout where they were small-boned, guileless where they were crafty, possessed of a flat, moon face framed with black hair that fell on either side like the strands of a mop. She had been born at an awkward time in China's modern history and was part of the "lost" generation that had had virtually no schooling. She had spent nearly two decades in barley fields near the Siberian border after being required to "go down" to the countryside. Her parents had counselled her not to marry there, because that would ruin her chances of moving back to Beijing, with the result that Swallow now found herself in her late thirties with no husband and no education. She had almost no chance of accessing the usual routes to America: graduate school or marriage. Yet Swallow radiated serenity. This was born of the failure to observe her surroundings, for Swallow was intellectually dim.

The parents disappeared. Swallow sat McKinley down and demonstrated *qigong* exercises. Her stomach smoothed out her sweater like a pink-and-black woolly spinnaker pinioned at four corners by her arms and legs. When she breathed in, the arc of her chest plumped like the breast of a feathery bird. She arched back, a perfect disc, a happy moon from a Chinese woodcut. Then she fluttered her hands from the wrists and brought her head back to centre. "This is the flying goose," she said. "Here you release bad *qi*."

Captain Wei and his wife emerged with a metal dish with four kidney-shaped sections that held peanuts, slices of meat in soy sauce, candied hawthorns, and crescents of preserved egg. Steaming platters of dumplings and a bottle of sweet wine followed.

"Shall I go to the Green Jade Hills?" Swallow had switched on her tape recorder, which played her own voice reading over a pizzicato on the *erhu*. McKinley stabbed a dumpling, taking advantage of the distraction to forgo trying to balance the slippery dough between his delicate, lacquered chopsticks. Captain Wei spooned two more dumplings onto McKinley's saucer. His wife's shining, squirrel's eyes were fixed in space somewhere above where the tape recorder stood on a velveteen cloth draped over the sideboard.

"When the sorrowful wind blows."

"Please correct my pronunciation," Swallow called over the tape.

"It's lovely," McKinley said. Her intonation, sliding up and down with a logic all its own, made it sound as if she were reading the poem from aboard a speeding train. "Are these your own poems?"

Swallow and her mother simultaneously put three fingers in front of their lips to cover a laugh. "Oh no," Swallow said. "By a very famous Tang poet."

The tape recorder switched itself off, and the four of them sat silently for a few minutes, picking at their food. McKinley was still ravenously hungry, but the others had stopped eating. "You certainly have worked hard at learning English," he said.

"Oh no, no, no," said Swallow a little too emphatically. "I am very far away."

McKinley did not know how he should answer this, so he smiled and took a sip of the very sweet wine. The captain's wife spoke inaudibly to her husband.

"My wife wants to know whether you know 'Onward Christian Soldiers'," Captain Wei said.

"Not all the words, I'm afraid."

Captain Wei's wife pushed back her chair and stood. Standing, she was only as tall as McKinley when he was hunkered over his little stool. She held her elbows bent and cupped her hands one inside the other, with the palms facing up. She fixed her odd, animal's eyes on a far corner of the room and opened her mouth to sing.

"Onward Christian soldiers, marching as to war, with the cross of Jesus, going on before."

"My wife is a Baptist," explained Captain Wei.

"Forward into battle, see their banners go."

"More wine?" said Captain Wei.

McKinley understood the religious fervour demonstrated by the captain's wife to be a sort of code, like sonar sent out from a submarine, intended to signal that these were friendly waters, where the grammar of Western business would be recognised.

Captain Wei tried to introduce the main topic of the evening, which was his plan to procure and resell catalytic converters. He had a friend attached to a factory that was making samples for export markets but had no access to potential importers abroad. The factory had briefed Captain Wei on the virtues of their converters, and he had several samples at home. In the evening, he would turn one in his hands, admiring the intricate ceramic honeycomb and imagining all the foreigners who would drive around in their cars, unaware that one critical component tucked inside the exhaust system had been made by Chinese hands.

McKinley avoided the discussion and excused himself at the earliest possible moment, but he could not escape being drawn into the catalytic converter plan or the more general schemes of the Wei family. Swallow insisted on walking him out to find a taxi, telling him that construction pits in the area could be treacherous to those who did not know the area. She held his elbow as they walked and spoke to him with heightened intimacy. "Someday I will tell you my story," she said, "but not now. It is very difficult for a foreigner to understand the situation of a single woman in China, but I am willing to tell you. It is a sad, sad story." McKinley nodded in the dark. They said goodbye at the edge of the Second Ring Road. "I hope you will come often to my family."

"I'm sure I will be back some day," McKinley said.

"Thank you," Swallow said. "When?"

"When?"

"When will you come next to my home?"

"Well, sometime soon, I suppose."

"Thursday? Are you free?"

McKinley shifted. "I'm not sure. I'll have to check."

"I'll call you Wednesday," she said, and they parted.

Alone in his bed, McKinley dreamed of the time when his older daughter had fallen into the small, ornamental pond in the back yard of their home in Michigan during winter, when it had a crust of ice. Marianne had lunged through the back door and jumped into the freezing water to retrieve her, finding herself so disoriented by the cold that she could only thrash. McKinley arrived later and waited, for seconds only but calmly, for the heads to surface then pulled them both out. He carried the girl inside and wrapped her in a blanket as Marianne limped and shivered by his side. Weeks later, the event became a party narrative for McKinley about the seconds in which life might have changed irrevocably. Marianne's narrative remained unarticulated; its substance was her husband's dispassionate seconds at the edge of the pool. She wondered whether he had a back-up plan.

After the dinner with McKinley, Captain Wei's wife impressed upon her husband the need to accelerate things with the American. Establishing an importing firm in America was the key to their plans for building a future for Swallow. In America, she could not only have an income but find a husband; Americans were always marrying in their thirties. Captain Wei decided he would bring McKinley to visit the factory in Hebei, and he felt sure that McKinley would be sufficiently impressed to commit to getting the big American auto companies to buy.

Swallow called on Wednesday, and McKinley made an excuse, but when Captain Wei telephoned on Thursday, McKinley agreed to go to Hebei out of inertia.

At dawn the next Saturday morning, Captain Wei and his driver waited outside McKinley's apartment building. Out came McKinley, tilted back as if weighted by his satchel and using his large, round belly as a ballast, with wiry arms and low-slung belt, a thin man hiding inside a portly one. His curls lay damp in fat little tendrils on his brow, like a baby's fingers, and his jaw was set in his habitual bright, feral expression. Swallow had come with her father as "interpreter", although McKinley's Chinese was much better than her English. Her mother had suggested this, since Captain Wei had mentioned that McKinley lived alone and therefore appeared available. Now McKinley was certain that Captain Wei was preparing a retirement package for him – Chinese wife, Chinese business.

They set out for Shijiazhuang. Captain Wei handed him a brochure whose first page showed the manager of the factory sitting behind an enormous wooden desk as if behind the poop deck of a ship. The manager's hands were folded and rested on the desk like a schoolboy's. McKinley leafed through subsequent pages showing a row of boxy machines that had something to do with manufacturing parts and a warehouse with boxes on shelves. In one picture, the factory's honeycomb was encased in a metal exhaust pipe. McKinley suspected that the picture had been taken from another company's brochure.

"This is the Hebei Express," said Captain Wei, as the car exited the long ramp to the highway. The road was perfectly empty, due to exorbitant tolls. "COSCO built the food concessions," he continued. "They are the most capital-intensive rest stops in the world. We wanted a first-class highway."

Indeed, the rest areas came along every fifteen miles or so, and each was themed for a different world monument: the Pyramids, the Eiffel Tower, the Parthenon. Chinese people didn't travel much, after all. When McKinley expressed interest in a men's room, Swallow took it upon herself to ensure his rapid relief, and the driver careened into the Castle on the Rhine rest area. The enormous front doors, made of reflective blue-glass panels, were loosely secured with a bicycle lock. McKinley wondered whether the river of blue-yellow gasoline and fetid water in front of the door intentionally simulated a moat. He walked around back to find a private place to relieve himself. There was a partition standing perpendicular to the Castle's back wall, and the ground on the other side was littered with filth. McKinley chose to stand outside the partition and aimed onto a cigarette butt.

The persistent ugliness of China wore him down. On returning to the car, he maliciously told Swallow that her hair looked especially beautiful swept back as it was today. In fact, come to think of it, she looked like a Rhine princess. Or perhaps a Wagnerian princess. Did she know Wagner? McKinley thought that a horned helmet would be perfect for Swallow. Swallow simpered with pleasure.

On to Shijiazhuang! They rode into town like Caesar crossing the Rubicon. The black Audi slowed to a stately crawl through the dusty streets, and the slogans painted on the sides of chemical factories set in fields seemed to stand in for welcoming banners held by town folk: *Serve the People! Socialism Is Good! Japanese Foreign Direct Investment Is Welcome!*

On through the gates of the auto-parts factory with imaginary garlands littering the hood of the car. The gatekeeper had been expecting them. They came to a halt in a semicircular driveway. The driver hopped out and extended his hands over the hinge of the door to help McKinley out while Captain Wei pushed a little from the inside. "I can manage," said McKinley.

The party that had gathered for their arrival grew, as their progression to the Foreign Guests Meeting Room continued. McKinley glanced up at the high, grease-smeared window at the far end of the hall, which glowed an incongruous rich orange, like coals in the belly of a furnace, due to the grit swirling through the air outside. The hall was draped in dusk. The wind outside bowed the trees into the ground, and grains of sand filtering through the air tinted the sky yellow. The mustard light seemed to bestow heightened significance to this Saturday morning, because it focused McKinley's attention momentarily beyond the meeting he was about to attend. The deep-hued light gave this cheap windowpane the solemnity of stained glass, as if the group were in procession to the apse of a cathedral.

The woman with the keys to the Foreign Guests Meeting Room was found and teacups were placed on the table. Then, to show that the factory was in step with the times, an assistant produced bottles of mineral water and packets of dried, salted plums. McKinley said a few words in Mandarin to establish his credentials and then let Swallow translate, since translation provided for an air of gravity and gave Swallow a role. McKinley asked for a pen and received one cased in cloisonné, just for foreign guests.

Captain Wei was clearly the man of culture in this group. He draped one elegant arm over the back of his chair, crossed his legs, and lit a cigarette, cradling the smoking elbow in his other arm. He affected an air of slight amusement. The factory director, earnest, stout, and forty (this was a factory that promoted "young cadres"), presented, as his six colleagues around the table studied the guests.

"Our exports are increasing fifteen per cent each year since the Opening and Reform," translated Swallow. "This is a Key Enterprise of Hebei Province."

The factory director stood to turn on an overhead projector. He rose like a full moon in front of the table, extending pinguid fingers before the screen to indicate slices of a pie chart that depicted the product mix at the factory. McKinley took off his glasses for the pleasure of seeing the factory director blur into pale fractals – blue lapels, white shirt, shimmery socks with black piping. The factory had been established shortly after Liberation. In 1995, it was named a Provincial Key Enterprise in Support of China's Third Pillar Industry, autos. Vice Premier Li Lanqing himself had visited. The famous American enterprise TRW had sent a delegation. The factory had formed an Equity Joint Venture with another Famous Enterprise, Eaton Corporation. Swallow's translation added immeasurably to the presentation.

McKinley wondered whether his own retirement would be like the homecoming in the movie *Gladiator*, a slow-motion run down a path on which olive trees encroached, strong breeze, a gate opening, the Elysian Fields. He pushed back his chair and stood to walk out of the room.

Captain Wei, the factory director, and Swallow all started towards him. "Are you uncomfortable?" said Captain Wei. "Should we pause?"

"Pour a cup of water for our foreign guest!" he called out to a tea attendant.

McKinley turned on his heel and surveyed the tabled gathering, savouring the startled attention. *Romans, friends, and countrymen, hear me for my cause!* He replaced his glasses on his nose and addressed the factory director.

"Do you have any fucking idea what you're talking about?" he said in Chinese to ensure full understanding. "Do you think you are fooling anyone with this shithole factory? Obviously, you make nothing of value. How would you become a 'key enterprise' without spending all your time and revenue on wining and dining corrupt officials? Why do you have so many 'leaders' at this limping factory in the middle of a field in Hebei? You probably earn all your money processing import permits for the Famous Foreign Enterprises for a fee. That's if you're not running karaoke bars and prostitution rings. Do you imagine that foreign markets are as stupid and corrupt as this one? Exports? Catalytic converters for North America? This is a sick joke. I'm going back to Beijing."

McKinley walked out, imagining the slack-jawed gathering at the table. He heard Captain Wei say, "I'll talk to him. He hasn't been feeling well." He followed McKinley into the hall, trailed by his daughter. He looked as if he would cry.

"Not feeling well?" said McKinley. "I was feeling very well until you tried to prostitute your imbecile daughter and use me to help you siphon money from this factory to keep you in brandy in your retirement." He was enjoying himself for the first time in months. "It is appalling. The whole episode makes me want to throw up." McKinley gestured with his finger at his throat. By now, they had reached the main entrance, and the driver was hovering. "Find me a cab!" raged McKinley. "I will pay American dollars, 300 of them, to get out of this hellhole." Instead, Captain Wei issued instructions and the black Audi took McKinley, alone, back to Beijing.

LOVE CHILD

"I always have the shrimp scampi and a tropical smoothie," Doudou told me. She didn't have to look at the menu. Doudou and her friends had been coming to Cheesecake Factory every Sunday of the school year. Nyack's mall was apparently the sentinel recreational activity for the school, which arranged a shuttle bus for the students every week, provided they had finished their homework. All children of wealthy Chinese families, they had fat allowance accounts, so they were not limited to only window shopping at the electronics or sporting goods stores. On my visit, the Nyack mall was the only place Doudou wanted to go, so here we were, she to shop and me to pay the bill. We had started by fortifying ourselves with lunch. I ate about half of my small salad and drank several cups of coffee as I watched her attack the ceramic boat of shrimp nearly afloat in a sea of butter. I hate Cheesecake Factory, but Doudou is my best friend's daughter. He's in China, she's in Nyack, New York, and I had promised him I'd look in on her.

Just two nights before, I had got a WeChat text from Liming: "If you get a chance, can you visit my daughter?" But Liming had only a son, so I thought. I texted him back: *where do I find her?* He sent the address of this boarding school in Nyack, and I took the day off from work to drive down there. Liming, after all, had helped me through a dozen crises. I was only too happy to be able to return a favour.

I friended Doudou on WeChat to announce that I was coming, and that led her mother to friend me, so I saw all the mother's "moments" posts, showing off the new mink stole Liming had given her, displaying bottles of vintage red wine she had bought, boasting about winning 8,000 renminbi at *mah jiang*, and whimsically posing, hips cocked and fingers in a V sign, against various cartoon backgrounds that added cat's ears and a whiskered nose or substituted her face for that of a cute panda. The mother was in her mid-thirties, which meant she had had Doudou when she was around twenty and Liming would have been over fifty.

Even with the GPS, it took me some time to find the school. There was no street address, and the campus was buried in more farmland than I knew existed in Nyack. Guernsey cows milled about on sloped, rocky pastures. I drove past the entrance several times but finally realised that the property with a high chain-link fence must be the school. I pulled up to a gate across the access road and pressed a button for the speaker. I had already registered online, a process that required submitting a recent photo and my number plate. A white mechanised camera aimed at my face and flashed. Something buzzed, and the gate opened.

The drive was about a half mile long. Uniformed guards carrying automatic weapons appeared on either side of the dirt road, walking beside the car as if to escort me. At the end of the access road was a parking lot next to three low-slung buildings plus a basketball court on which Chinese boys were shooting hoops, wearing uniform white pants and royal blue sweaters bearing a crest. Girls in similar uniforms, but with skirts and knee socks instead of pants, squatted by the court. In China, I thought, they would have been in unisex sweatsuits, but here they took on the look of a British public school.

I parked my Prius next to a Mercedes coupe. Most of the lot was filled with Land Rovers and Lexus SUVs, uniformly black. The students probably thought I was applying for a janitorial position. I got out and followed an arrow on a wooden sign with carved white letters: *Visitors This Way to the Office* and walked along a woodchip path that led to reception. Inside an attendant sat in a reception booth behind a window made of thick, fogged glass with holes arranged in a circle for speaking, like the window at a check-cashing company. I had to bend down to get my mouth close to the speaking area.

"I'm here to see Han Dou," I said. "My name is Bai Li. I made an appointment." Since everyone here was Chinese, I spoke Chinese. It felt like being in Beijing.

The receptionist flipped pages in a large appointment

book.

"Can I see your ID?"

I gave her my American passport, which she kept.

"I'll call Doudou. You have permission to take her out this afternoon."

I sat on the couch in the reception area and waited. Students walked through in pairs. One was twirling a basketball on his forefinger. Pretty soon, a slim, homely young girl in the white-and-blue uniform, but with fancy running shoes, presented herself.

"Uncle?"

"Are you Doudou?" I said, standing up. She was half a head taller than I and probably half my weight. "I'm happy to meet you. You look just like your father."

Doudou just blinked, as if in a snowstorm. "The dorm monitor said I could go out with you today."

"Well, let's go then."

Once in my Prius, I asked her where she wanted to go, and she gave me directions to Nyack Crystal Mall. This was one of those suburban constructions that might have been used as a model for a spaceship in a movie about whole colonies travelling through space for hundreds of years: multilevel, colonnaded, imposing, and surrounded by wasteland. Inside, the mall felt like a "Death Star", with four storeys of catwalks crossing the atrium and aluminium casing on the steel girders separating the floors.

Doudou's resemblance to Liming was remarkable: the same half-closed eyes, the same skinny build, the mouth with ironically upturned corners. She even wore little round glasses like his and had the same thin hair and blunt-cut bangs. She was a female, fifty-year-younger version of Liming. Doudou sat in the booth at Cheesecake Factory scarfing down the shrimp with slice after slice of crusty Italian bread, which she slathered with a half inch of the butter she had specifically requested, and I wondered how she could tuck all this food into her string bean frame. I tried to remember whether Liming had been like this as well, but back when we were teenagers, no one in China even had meat more than twice a month, let alone bread with slabs of butter.

"How's your dad?" I asked in Chinese. I was surprised that, despite two years at boarding school in America, she did not seem to speak any English.

"Super busy. He's only home in Beijing about two nights a month. He's always travelling."

This made me unsure whether Doudou thought that Liming was married to her mother and just travelled a lot, while I knew that he had a home with a wife and son and did not actually travel outside the city very much. I didn't pursue it.

I paid for lunch then spent two hours following Doudou into stores, where she chose two iPods, a pair of running shoes, two oversized sports jerseys, and running shorts, and I put it all on my credit card. Doudou wasn't at all shy about imposing these expenditures on me, although she didn't insist when she wanted a laptop and I was unenthusiastic. After I'd spent nearly $700, I suggested we take a break for coffee.

"How do you like school?" I asked, trying to keep the conversation generic.

"I hate it." She did not elaborate. "Can we get a pumpkin spice frappuccino? Venti. And a chocolate muffin."

I ordered the food along with a brewed coffee for

myself and watched Doudou consume the muffin.

"Why do you hate school?"

"It's stupid, being stuck out here. My father's going to transfer me to a school in Washington. There's much more to do there."

"Do you like the classes?"

"They're okay."

"What's your favourite?"

"I guess I like physics. Most girls like language or history."

"They do?"

"Sure." She was scrolling though Instagram photos on her phone while we were speaking. I don't think she looked at me once. She had a case that made her phone look like it had big pink mouse ears. I wondered whether she would recognise me if we met outside, but I realised that even if she stared straight at me for a couple of hours, she probably wouldn't.

"Thing is, the Chinese literature teacher in this school molests all the girl students, so they don't like to be in his class. One girl killed herself."

"What?! When did that happen? Did anyone tell the authorities?"

After a short pause, I continued, "Is the teacher still there?"

"Nah, it would ruin the school's reputation. Could you imagine if the parents heard that a teacher was a paedophile, and that a girl killed herself because she couldn't stand him? Might as well close the school tomorrow."

"So they just covered it up?"

"Yeah, teenagers kill themselves all the time. They just

said she had mental problems."

I finished my coffee. "Do you want to go someplace else? Maybe see a movie?"

"I want to go to Dick's Sporting Goods."

"Okay."

"I have to get a jersey for a friend."

We went to Dick's, and Doudou picked out some sports team's jersey. I paid $85. I thought, I could get something just like that for $10, but I didn't say it. I wondered whether all the kids in this school were like Doudou, stranded in Nyack, never seeing their families, whose parents gave them so much spending money that $85 for a jersey was nothing special. We visited a couple more stores and, finally, Doudou said she wanted to go back to her dorm. She had homework to do. I drove her the short distance back to the school. It was raining, and I didn't get out of the car to see her inside. The students were walking in pairs along the woodchip path towards the cafeteria, and Doudou hurried over so she would not miss dinner. Doudou turned and gave a small wave, raising three shopping bags dangling from her wrist. I started the three-hour drive home.

I reported to Liming that his daughter was doing well in school and spoke very good English. I didn't ask him how he came to have a daughter; there was nothing for him to tell. Liming is nothing special to look at and was always shy with girls. He is like a pre-pubescent child in the body of a seventy-year-old man. His wife is a harpy who is constantly dissatisfied with him. But Liming had made a fortune in real estate, and rich always trumps good-looking. Liming has always had a knack for exploiting loopholes in systems that others find impenetrable. While I was still biking every day to the Foreign Languages Press and working on translating Chinese classics into Hindi, Liming was being driven around in a Mercedes. He bought a huge, pink-tile mansion on the east side of the city, and he sent his son, who was not a gifted student, to a private boarding school. Liming's wife had quit her job, since it was inappropriate for the wife of such a wealthy man to be working. Bored without her son around, she constantly complained about Liming. I understood why he would have taken up with someone younger and more pliant. Once Doudou's mother got pregnant, Liming would have installed her in her own house and taken care of her monthly expenses. It's awkward, though, to have a love child in one's own city. Better to send her to boarding school overseas.

I did not hear from Doudou again, but I followed her mother's posts with morbid interest. Most were about her little white dog, Lulu. She dressed Lulu in a sailor's uniform and held up a paw in salute. She posted videos of Lulu apparently dreaming, because she'd bark in her sleep and thrash her paws around angrily. She wrote posts about cooking spaghetti for Lulu.

Liming did not communicate much. On holidays, he sent digital greeting cards that I suspected he forwarded from others. Then, towards Christmas, he sent me another message about Doudou.

"Brother, I need you to look in on Doudou again. I've transferred her to a school in Washington. Is that near you? I need you to pick her up and put her on a plane back to Beijing."

I live in Rochester, and Washington, DC, is a long drive, but, as I said, I owe a lot to Liming. I got the address from Doudou, told her I'd be there the next afternoon, and set out in my Prius. This time, I didn't think to call ahead to register my visit.

The school turned out to be in Hyattsville, Maryland, a remote part of Washington. Like the school in Nyack, this school seemed to want to emulate British public schools. It was called The Grange. A group of girls in uniform skirts was playing lacrosse on a field above the administration building. A coat of arms painted on a wooden shield was hung over the main entrance.

This reception area lacked the check-cashing vibe of Doudou's first school. There was a sofa and two armchairs covered in chintz under a replica Tiffany lamp shaped like a large, wilted flower with petals of coloured glass. A young woman sat at a polished-wood desk with an old-fashioned, touch-tone phone. I told her I was there to see Han Dou, a ninth grader. She corrected me: second form. I went back to the sofa to wait.

Instead of Doudou, a woman in her late thirties came out and introduced herself.

"I'm Dr Li," she said, shaking my hand. "I understand you're Miss Han's uncle."

"Yes." There was no point explaining how tentative my relationship with her really was.

Dr Li was elegantly dressed in a solid-blue shift. Her hair was pulled back, exposing small gold studs in her ears. She smelled of baby powder and exuded calm authority. Despite being at least thirty years older than Dr Li, I felt awkward around her, as if I were the student and she the teacher. I didn't know what had happened with Doudou, but I already felt defensive.

"You can rest assured that we have not involved the police," she began. I must have looked alarmed, because she cocked her head and looked at me curiously. "You haven't heard about the fire?"

"No, I haven't heard about a fire. Doudou's father asked me to come get her, so here I am. No one has told me why."

"Why don't we go to my office, where we can be more comfortable?"

I followed Dr Li, who swiped the ID card hanging around her neck to open the door to a corridor lined with other doors. We went into her office and sat in facing armchairs. She made me a cup of instant coffee.

"Doudou came to us at the beginning of the school year. She was highly recommended, and as you know, her father has considerable influence. So we were happy to have her.

"Doudou is quite a good student," she continued. I suspected that school administrators used these same words with the parents of all the unremarkable students. "She seemed happy here, and she settled right into the dormitory and made friends. But small things started to go missing – one student's earrings, a teacher's fountain pen. We suspected it was Doudou, but instead of accusing her, we had her meet with me and talk through her anxiety about blending in. My job is to look after students who are experiencing distress.

"We met each morning before class. I felt she was becoming more open with her feelings, more articulate, and generally happier. But then a bird that one of the sixth-grade teachers kept in the classroom was found dead. It was a very handsome parrot, kind of a mascot, that the students adored. Someone had fastened a cord around its neck, tied one end to the cage, then opened the door to let the bird fly out. The cord got tighter and tighter around the poor thing's neck, and the more it struggled to get away, the tighter the slipknot became, until the bird asphyxiated itself.

"Any one of the students could have got access, and anyone could have done it. I thought initially that one of the younger students may have been trying to do something nice for Billy – that was the parrot's name – and didn't realise that tying a string around its neck would be fatal. Once the bird died, the student would have been too embarrassed to admit fault."

"So why do you think it was Doudou?"

"She has a secretive streak. When I brought up the parrot during one of our morning sessions, Doudou laughed, and given the laugh and the disingenuous way she claimed not to know anything about it, I felt sure that Doudou had killed Billy and had done it on purpose.

"Still, I could not be 100 per cent certain, and so I kept it to myself. I just became wary around Doudou. I started to notice how she acted with her classmates, playing basketball, in the cafeteria. There was something very unsettling about her. She takes pleasure in hurting people. Small things. Once I saw her in the hall between classes. There's a girl who's a bit awkward. She has a hormonal disturbance and is very small-statured, maybe the height of a ten-year-old. She's self-conscious and has trouble making friends. I suppose she must have attached herself to Doudou, because when she saw Doudou down the hall, she lit up and started waving and calling. Doudou returned the greeting enthusiastically. She smiled and waved and started over towards Linda. But then she walked straight past her, pretending she was waving to someone else entirely. I could see Linda's face just crumple with disappointment.

"Another time, on the basketball court, a group of girls was playing a friendly game after dinner. I saw Doudou intentionally trip the girl who was guarding her, then help her up as if the girl had just stumbled.

"I noted all these things and I developed some concern for Doudou. I just guessed she was lonely, perhaps neglected by her family, a little bit lost in America. But then the fires started."

"What do you mean? Are you saying Doudou started fires in the school?"

"There have been a series of mysterious fires near the school, initially quite small. There was a brushfire in a patch of woods off the Beltway that no one connected with the school or our students. The fire department was able to put it out in a few minutes.

"Next there were a couple of fires in trash cans in the centre of Hyattsville. Doudou was never accused of setting them, but both happened on Saturday nights, when Doudou had a pass and had gone downtown.

"The last straw was a fire last Sunday in the school's stables. Fortunately, we caught it early enough that we saved the horses, and only a small part of the stable burned down. But it could have killed our horses. If the fire had spread, it could have killed people as well."

"That is a very serious accusation. I mean if you really think Doudou did that, you should report her to the police."

Dr Li cocked her head and examined me as if I had

said there were recording devices in my teeth.

"We're a Chinese school. We take care of our problems ourselves," she said. "That is why we asked her father to remove her from the school."

Liming had not told me if he had further plans for his daughter. All I could do was pack up her things and bring her back with me to Rochester. We drove most of the way in silence, as Doudou scrolled through posts on her phone and listened to music with earbuds. But I was too curious about the arson.

"Did you really set fire to the stables?" I asked.

"Yeah."

The answer was so matter-of-fact that I was taken aback.

"Why?"

"No reason."

"There has to be a reason."

"I like fires. Doesn't everybody?"

I considered this. "Yes, I think people like fires. But they generally light them in their fireplaces. You destroyed valuable school property and risked getting arrested."

"My dad would never let me get arrested. And he can pay them to build a new stable. He won't even miss the money."

Doudou stayed with us for three days, while I arranged for her to fly back to China. Liming gave little instruction. When I telephoned him, he whispered that I should text him, because he was with his wife. I gathered that she still didn't know about Doudou and her mother. So I bought Doudou a ticket home and texted the information to Liming, who said he would arrange a car to pick her up at the airport. When I gave Doudou the flight information, she texted her mother that she would be returning and showed me the WeChat message she received in response, full of smile emojis: *Great! The door will be unlocked. I have my* mah jiang *game on Sunday, but I'll be back around dinner time.*

On Saturday, I piled Doudou's things into the car and again set out on a long drive, this time to Newark, where she could get on a direct flight to Beijing, because I was not at all sure that Doudou could be trusted to transfer flights on her own. She wore a beret of white imitation fur and a matching jacket with pom-poms on strings, and she clutched the mouse-ear phone. As she walked into security, she turned with her sleepy, half-closed Liming eyes and gave me a wink.

BODY SNATCHER

His father had died, and Lu wanted me to arrange the funeral. That alarmed me. Why wouldn't he handle it himself? In the past, Lu had dropped what he was doing every time his father's pancreatic cancer took a turn for the worse, which had been often. Now he was too busy to handle a funeral. Something was wrong. Lu was also whispering on the phone, as if his father's death needed to be a secret. When I said I wanted to see him, instead of responding, he handed the phone to his wife.

"Lu's in the hospital," Mei said in a whisper.

"What? Where? What happened? I'll be right there."

"It's his heart. Look, it's fine, really. You don't need to come. In fact, it's better if you don't."

I let the silence between us sit for a minute.

"When did this happen? He never had a heart condition before."

"It only just came up."

"I want to see him. Why aren't you telling me where he is?"

Lu and I are in our early forties. He is my oldest friend. We are the sort of opposites who attract. He is short and fat, with earlobes that stick out like rudders, a dark-red complexion, and heavily lidded eyes, like a turtle's. He takes great pleasure in pulling something over on people who take themselves seriously, and he seeks out risk. As for me, I'm thin and cautious. I've worn glasses since I was in primary school, and I have thin hair, buck teeth, and small eyes. I try not to be noticed, while Lu loves attention.

When we were growing up, our families lived in the same alley in Beijing, and we attended the same schools all the way until college. When we were teenagers, on Saturday afternoons after our cram class we would wheel around the city's back alleys on our bicycles and stop for a "snowball" cone, a ball of frozen vanilla ice cream with chocolate coating packed into a soggy cone, all for what was then the royal sum of sixty cents. These had appeared on street stands to replace the frozen red-bean or green-pea ice pops that had sold for a penny or two. Our parents would not have approved spending the exorbitant sum, and that is partly what we liked about the cones.

In the late 1990s, when I went to university, Lu went straight into business and made unimaginable money for the time. He assembled smuggled TVs, invested it in a coal mine, put money into a blueberry farm, tried distributing medical equipment, and along the way, he married Mei, an intelligent but depressive girl who reminded me of an Edward Gorey character. Mei had long periods when she stayed in their apartment playing solitaire on a desktop computer. She had a long face, stringy hair she let fall in front of her eyes, and a lugubrious manner. She let her sleeves droop over her hands and always wore black. I, on the other hand, married a cheerful, well-adjusted girl who is as unremarkable as I am. She has an online shop selling ceramics and travels frequently to Jingdezhen to buy the items she resells at a mark-up. We don't want children. We have a pleasant, one-bedroom apartment in Haidian. We alternate Sundays with her parents and mine. It's an uneventful and unsurprising life.

I asked Mei again where Lu was. The secrecy around his health was becoming alarming.

"I'm trying to keep his location confidential," she said. "It's for his own safety." I could hear Mei sniffling on the other end of the phone.

"Where are you, Mei? I'll meet you."

We agreed to meet for dinner, and she gave me the name of a restaurant in the southern part of the city, an ugly district whose grey high-rises made it easy to feel anonymous: I couldn't imagine running into anyone I knew there. I arrived at six and found Mei had already taken a table at the back near the bathrooms, even though there were plenty of nicer tables along the front windows. She was wearing quilted pyjamas with pictures of bears in nightcaps and dressing gowns. Over the pyjamas she wore a bomber jacket and, on her feet, faux leather boots.

"What's with the outfit?"

"I'm actually staying in the hospital too." Patients in Chinese hospitals often wear pyjamas from home. Since stays are lengthy – often weeks or months – patients tend to leave only for meals or to run errands. You often see them standing outside hospital gates smoking cigarettes.

"Why are you in the hospital? Are you sick?"

"No, it's just the easiest way for us both to stay out of sight for a while."

This made sense to me. A hospital can be a place of refuge, where public officials go when they fall out of favour, to weather a political storm, or where fugitives gain a few days of respite from the law, like in churches in the West.

"Why do you need to do that?"

"It's complicated."

She briefly told me the story of her husband's distress. His latest company hired itself out to small banks to fix their books ahead of bureaucratic audits. Lu knew just enough about accounting to produce plausible-looking books, and he had a team of accountants working with him.

At a recent audit, he had run into some bad luck.

The Houshayu Commercial Bank had retained Lu to get its accounts repaired in time for the annual "big" audit by high-level regulators. Borrowers were delinquent, and the bank was dangerously short of cash. Tellers had quietly been given instructions not to allow withdrawals of more than five thousand renminbi but to make an excuse and tell depositors they could come back. The mid-level manager who hired Lu's company was clearly very anxious. But equally, banks will pay a lot to get out of this sort of jam, and Lu and Mei hoped to get a windfall.

"So, what happened?"

"Well, he had to find nearly eighty million to pour into the bank's accounts overnight. Lu found a grey-market lender, but the loan came with a fee of two per cent overnight, paid in advance."

I whistled. "That's 1.6 renminbi."

"Yeah. It was a lot of money. And the bank had to transfer the money back as soon as the auditors had signed off."

"So the transfer went wrong?" I asked.

Mei went on. "The bank gets a surprise visit by a delegation from the city regulators. It seems there's a big new investment coming in, and they have to make sure everything is on the up-and-up."

A delegation of government officials, dressed alike in dark slacks, pastel golf shirts, and tasselled loafers, had gathered in the lobby as the bank manager sat at a terminal to demonstrate new banking software. The eighty million hit the accounts just as the manager signed in and opened the accounts interface. The visiting delegation watched in real time as the value of consumer deposits flipped on the screen like cherries and lemons on a slot machine. This was too obvious even for the bank manager, who acted shocked. The regulators immediately ordered him to freeze all accounts.

"I guess that means they couldn't transfer the eighty million back to the lender?"

"Right, and the guy who lent them the money is in charge of interbank loans at a big state bank. He's really worried, so he goes and hires a gang of thugs to collect."

"What about the bank manager who hired Lu? Is he helping?"

"Head in the sand. The guy is an army veteran who was assigned this job when he was demobilised. He doesn't know anything about banking, and he also doesn't understand how dangerous fixing the accounts can be. He is totally stunned when two men visit him and tell him he needs to find a way to unfreeze the funds, or his wife and child might not be safe."

She took a drag on her Hongtashan.

"It gets worse." Mei described how, one week later, when the funds had not been unfrozen, the manager's wife answered a knock on the door at dinnertime. The couple's teenage daughter heard a popping sound, went into the living room, and found her mother dead by the front door. She had been shot in the face.

"The girl had to see her mother with just a bloody hole where her eye had been."

"Wow, that's horrible. Did the guy make a police report?"

"Are you kidding? At least he's sensible enough not to do that. These mobs are all connected to the police."

Mei felt it was only a matter of time before the lender and his enforcers would get to Lu. She was terrified.

"We'll figure this out. Trust me," I said, without conviction.

We ordered another bottle of beer and a plate of tripe.

"Can't you just make a run for it?" I suggested. "Put Lu in the car and have you hide out at my place until the scandal dies down and the bank figures something out?"

"The mob will find us. They have our ID numbers and car registration. They'll interrogate our friends and stake out our place for as long as it takes. And after what happened to that manager's wife? I'd never open my front door again."

We paid the restaurant and drove to the "new economic zone", where Lu was in the hospital. About a hundred metres from the hospital entrance, Mei cut the headlights and parked the car on the sidewalk.

"Put your arm around me," she told me.

"Why? What's going on?"

She pointed to two men who were sitting on stools outside the hospital gate and playing a game that involved slapping down cards on an upended wooden stool that stood between them to serve as a makeshift table.

"They won't look carefully at me if it seems like we're together."

We walked into the hospital entrance as a couple. The men didn't look up from their card game.

"How do you know they're here for you and Lu?"

"They're off-duty police. I've seen them in uniform. These gangs always hire police, because police can make sure there's no investigation."

She snuggled her chin into my neck.

"I'm really worried they'll get sick of waiting and just gun him down inside the hospital. That stuff happens, you know."

"This is Beijing. They can't do just anything. And anyway, we will move quickly." I spoke with more conviction than I felt.

We took the stairs up three flights. Lu was in a hospital room with seven other men, all recovering from surgery. He put on a bathrobe and shoes and came into the hall, where we had a smoke and talked about how to get him out.

Lu seemed cheerful; he had always enjoyed the feeling of living on the edge of the law. We sat on the conjoined orange-plastic chairs in the hospital corridor, chain-smoking and trying to figure out a means of escape for

Lu. Lots of visitors were milling around.

"I can't even leave the building," he said. "I'm sure those two guys outside have been sent for me. Fortunately, they don't know that Mei is with me – she checked into the hospital under a different name."

"What if we get you a fake ID?"

"The police control all the fake IDs. To get a good one, you have to be connected to them, so these thugs would find out. I'm sure they're monitoring all the issuances right now."

I went out again to buy two litres of beer and some sunflower seeds. The two men were still slouched outside, now smoking and staring into space. They checked me out but quickly lost interest.

When I got back, Mei went to her own room to sleep, and Lu and I sat hunched on the seats, smoking and talking. He wore a puffy down jacket over his pyjamas; I had worn a leather-covered down jacket and long underwear, and even so, I was chilly.

I stayed in the hospital that night, afraid that the guard dogs outside might identify me as Lu's friend. I slept for a couple of hours slumped on the chair in the hallway and dreamed about hiding in the branches of a tree, holding my breath as police searched for me below.

In the morning, I got some breakfast with Mei at an outdoor stall. I said I would get Lu out of the hospital, but I told her nothing more. When I walked out of the hospital gate, the guard seemed to look at me questioningly. I ignored him, as I thought most visitors probably did; they would have been preoccupied with their sick relatives. I took the subway all the way to the end of Line 1 and went straight to the city crematorium they call Babaoshan.

I strode through the gate and into the main hall, where there was a registration desk. "Who is in charge?" I demanded. "I need to see the manager right away."

"What is this about?" asked the young woman at the desk.

"I am not going to waste my time telling you what this is about." I raised my voice in an attempt to act deliberately unreasonable. I wanted them to worry that I would disturb the lucrative business of providing a serene location for mourners to gather, and to send out a manager to keep me quiet. "You are holding my uncle's body illegally." In short order, a middle-aged man in a black suit with a white carnation in his lapel appeared.

"I'm Wang Ancheng's nephew," I said, adopting an indignant tone. This was Lu's father's name, and of course I had known him well. It was no stretch to call him an uncle. Since I happen to have the same surname as Lu, it was reasonable that Ancheng might be a brother of my own father. Tens of millions of people in China are named Wang.

"I need my uncle's body *immediately*. I know the body has not been cremated yet," I demanded.

"Perhaps you did not know," I went on, "because I would not suspect you of dishonouring a national minority. We are Huis." This of course was a lie, but I knew the suggestion that Ancheng had been Muslim would terrify the funeral director, since laws around protecting the rights of minorities to burial are very tightly enforced to compensate for the general discrimination in other arenas. "Our family is very religious, and we believe that Uncle Wang will not be with God if his body is destroyed. We never authorised the hospital to bring him here."

"Mr Wang, I'm so sorry for your loss, but your uncle did not have 'Hui' on his identity card. How could we have known? As you know, Chinese law requires cremation unless you have a special permit."

"If I had been given notice and the hospital had not simply carted my uncle's body away, I would have given notice. I wasn't going to apply for a burial permit while my uncle was still alive."

The attitude of indignation gave the manager pause.

"I know this is creating a lot of extra work for you," I said, softening my tone. "I appreciate all Babaoshan is doing for my family. I know you have already incurred significant expense for a casket and to prepare my uncle's body for viewing before cremation. I'd certainly like to support the institution's work." I took a roll of bills out of my pocket and peeled off twenty hundred-yuan notes.

This had the desired effect. The funeral director disappeared into the back for about ten minutes and returned with four young men who were carrying a pine casket with the body of Lu's father. I had hired a van, which was waiting in the courtyard of the complex. The four men shoved the casket into the back of the van. I thanked them and gave each a one-hundred-yuan note.

I had the driver take me to Mei and Lu's building in Wangjing, and I tipped him to help me carry the casket into their apartment; I had got the keys from Lu. We had a hard time in the elevator and had to tilt the casket diagonally. People milling around the courtyard of the building stared at us, but no one asked me what we were doing. On the eleventh floor, I opened the metal security door, and we pushed inside with the casket.

The air was stuffy and smelled like old cotton candy and, strangely, cats. No one had been there for months. The driver and I propped the casket against the couch. I thanked him and shut the door. Alone with the casket in the apartment, I made myself a large bowl of noodles and watched an old war movie on television, eyeing the pine box and imagining Lu's father inside, his skin drawn across the skeletal head, his eyes hollow.

In the evening, I went to visit a friend of Lu's to whom he'd given his old car. The car was still registered to Lu, since licence plates were not transferrable. I explained to the friend that Lu needed the car but that he would be back in Beijing soon and would make it up to him. "Lu would ask you himself, but he can't get away from work, and it's really important." Reluctantly, the friend gave me the keys to the cherry-coloured BYD and told me where to find it parked. I drove it back to Mei and Lu's place near Chaoyang Park. On the way, I filled the tank with gas.

I waited until after midnight when it was truly dark and there were few people abroad. I pried open the casket. Lu's father was dressed in a blue Sun Zhongshan suit. His body was rigid, but there was no putrefaction yet. I found a duvet in the closet and spread it on the floor then dumped the old man's body onto the coverlet and wrapped him up tight, tying up the bundle with twine. The hardest part was getting him into the elevator and then dragging him across the courtyard by myself. The old man had been eaten up by the disease and weighed very little, but he was rigid and surprisingly difficult to carry. I had to drag the body. Eventually, I managed to get his body to where I had parked the car, just outside the complex's gate.

I opened the driver's-side door and snipped the cords tying the duvet, yanking it away, so that the old man's body rolled into the car head-first. Heaving, I managed to lift the legs into the well in front of the driver's seat. His legs were planked diagonally, with his shoulders resting on the headrest. It had to do. I closed the door.

At the gas station, I had paid the attendant to let me fill a plastic container, saying I had to help a friend who had run out. Now I saturated a rag in gasoline, took the cap off the gas tank, and stuffed the rag in. I took out a length of cord that I planned to use as a fuse and drenched it with the gasoline then sprinkled the rest on the old man's body. I strung the heavy cord from the gas tank to the other side of the street. Then I used my lighter to set fire to the trail of gas. I ran as quickly as I could, and in an anxious minute or so, the car exploded.

When the firetruck arrived, I was back in the apartment. Like everyone else, I came outside and feigned curiosity. I did not speak with the police; I let them trace the licence plate and draw their conclusions.

Police verified that the car belonged to Lu, and they used DNA testing to confirm that he had died in the explosion. The national genetic database showed a match close enough that no one questioned the identity. There was an announcement in the paper. The police must have known that it was a case of arson, but Lu was famously in debt, and you never know what the gangs might be capable of. Better to keep it quiet.

THE GYM TEACHER

Lü Li and old Mrs Wang had met while walking their little Shih Tzu dogs, who were both called Doudou. The two old people had lost their spouses, Lü recently and Mrs Wang fifteen years earlier. Their relationship developed when Mrs Wang stopped by Lü Li's apartment to drop off a bag of cornmeal. Soon her visits became almost daily. She would leave a potted begonia he might enjoy, a goldfish in a plastic sack, or a sticky disc of *babaofan*, the sweet "eight treasures rice" filled with dates and lotus seeds that Northerners like to eat on holidays. She began to stay longer and longer, sometimes to mend Lü Li's clothes, sometimes to prepare an evening meal. He was grateful but quietly assumed that these favours were only his due as a single man. He could not be expected to care for himself as assiduously as a wife would. In due course, Mrs Wang moved in. They slept in the large bed he had shared with his wife, but each slept rolled chastely in a separate quilt, facing out, on either side of the bed. At night, they changed out of their clothes in the bathroom with the door shut.

Lü Li's attraction for women was a mystery to all his male friends. Even his name sounded to Chinese ears like "donkey". He had a long head with stupid, soft-brown eyes set so far apart that he could have stayed watchful while lifting his bowl up to his nose to shovel the rice into his mouth with chopsticks. He had long ears and a mouth that drooped comically at either side, all set atop a large, unwieldy body shaped like the cardboard box you might get a desk delivered in. When he opened his mouth to speak, what came out was more bray than human voice. And yet this man was catnip to women of every age. It may have been simply that he liked them.

Before he retired, Lü Li was a gym teacher by day and watchman by night. The company that employed him had offices next door to the high school where he taught gym, and it turned out that having a private place, behind locked gates, which his wife and daughters could not enter, was exactly what had been lacking in Lü Li's life.

His first adventure was with Ms Yu, an English teacher at the school who was then around menopausal age. She had tightly permed hair and a soft body like two feather pillows tied at the waist. Ms Yu had a husband who worked at a nearby printing plant and a teenage son who was not studying as much as he should be for the university exam that he would have to sit in a year's time. The little time her husband spent at home was taken up with "walking" his birds by swinging their shrouded cages back and forth, as they clung to their perches, thus exercising their little legs, and with watching football matches on television. Neither of these pastimes interested Ms Yu, and after her son grew into his teens and no longer required much care, she took up hobbies like painting and calligraphy, neither of which she was very good at. She was, however, diligent in practice. Her calligraphy remained uninteresting but in painting, she at least learned to paint the individual leaves on a stand of bamboo.

Ms Yu had not really noticed the gym teacher until one noontime when he was standing behind her in the refectory line. She dropped a white plastic saucer of pickles that clattered on the floor in smaller and smaller arcs, making a surprisingly loud sound that stopped the other faculty members' conversation as they watched the commotion. Lü Li crouched down to help her pick up the dish, and their fingers met for a moment that was, for her, electric.

"Thank you," she said, looking up into his eyes.

"No problem." He gripped the tip of her left ring finger and stroked it ever so slightly with his thumb. Ms Yu knew then that she would have sex with Lü Li the gym teacher.

He did not have to do much at all. She found reasons to go down to his office in the basement of the high school building, where he sat among footballs and collapsible netted goals. The room smelled of leather and cleaning fluid, which Ms Yu, who had never had an affair in her two decades of marriage, took to be the pinnacle of masculinity.

"I'm starting menopause," she said to him by way of explaining her flush.

He looked up from his desk, where he had been reading

a *Youth Daily* article about a Hong Kong movie star's marriage to a mainlander. "I love menopausal women." He went back to his reading. Soon she was calling him at home and hanging up when his wife answered the phone.

"I'm just leaving school," she said at seven one evening. "I had to work late. Do you want to come out and have a coffee?"

He was silent for a minute.

"I'm all sweaty from the basketball game. You wouldn't want me like this."

After two months of frustrating innuendo, she decided to confront him. "I guess it's a midlife thing. I can't get you out of my head."

Lü Li said nothing, but he called a friend who had suggested he take a night watchman job at the office next door to the school.

"Are you still looking to fill the job?" he said.

"Yes," said his friend. "But you need to stay there overnight. We can put a bed there for you."

Lü Li told his wife that this would be an ideal way to earn some extra money, which they would need to do now that their son was getting ready for college. Lü Li locked the gate at 10 p.m. Ms Yu the English teacher came at eleven and stayed for an hour.

Lü Li and Ms Yu got along well until her husband discovered their affair. Then, it turned out, she wanted to divorce her husband and marry Lü Li. Lü Li preferred to end it, but given that they worked at the same school, it was difficult to separate without histrionics. The night watchman job again became convenient; he no longer admitted her at eleven. He told her that the boss had said he was going to check up at night, and Lü Li could not take the chance of being discovered. At school, he ignored her on the excuse of needing to be discreet.

Then Lü Li began an affair with a senior student. The girl was leggy and skittish, and Lü Li liked her a lot. But he feared she would grow attached, and he knew it was not a good idea to sleep with a student. With some reluctance, he ended the affair.

Next, he took up with a flighty young assistant teacher who had just got out of teacher-training school and who affected the English name Nora. Nora was birdlike, with a fluty voice and an odd habit of carrying her arms in front of her with her hands dangling, as if begging for something. She wore thick glasses and seemed to have poor vision. She often stumbled. She seemed genuinely devoted to Lü Li and, when she saw him at school, beamed with genuine pleasure, showing gapped front teeth.

Nora did not last long at the school; she got a permanent job up in the western district of Huilongguan, which was near her apartment and, despite real affection for Lü Li, felt that the ninety-minute subway ride was impractical, and she broke it off. But Lü Li, surprising himself, had got attached to her. He persuaded Nora to come spend Saturday nights with him on the single bed in the office after the gate was locked. To sweeten the offer, he promised to take her out to hear music on the Sanlitun Bar Street before he had to lock up at ten.

Lü Li found himself thinking about the girl during the week, the rib cage that spread like a bird's, the spindly legs, the way she squinted at him as if his face held a puzzle. Her body smelled light and citrusy, not like the dense bready smell Ms Yu had had underneath her clothes.

Their arrangement worked well for three weeks. On

the fourth, a Sunday morning in early June, Lü Li and Nora woke late and basked in the lemony sun that had been so rare in the winter and spring months. Lü Li began to nibble her ear, and Nora placed a lazy, affectionate hand on his jaw and turned his face towards hers to kiss him. Then the door of the office opened and in walked the owner of the company Lü Li was charged with guarding. Mr Yang was followed by Lü Li's wife. Lü Li jumped up and grabbed his T-shirt from the straight-backed chair next to the bed, holding it in front of his groin. Nora sat up in bed and yanked the quilt up over her bony shoulders.

"I knew it!" his wife declared, as Mr Yang stood there looking awkward. "Never letting me come up here! I should have known what was going on from the very start."

Mr Yang looked down at his feet. He sidled over to where Nora was still sitting on the bed.

"Why don't you get yourself dressed and take off," he said to her quietly. "Old Lü has a lot to sort out."

Nora slipped out of the bed, picked up her clothes, and ran across the hall into the company meeting room, where she quickly pulled on her pants and her shoes, grabbed her little panda bag, and left the building.

The wife would not forgive Lü Li and insisted that he sleep in the day room. She made sarcastic remarks about his new interest in gymnastics. None of this bothered Lü Li much, as his goal was really to be left alone.

With Nora gone, Ms Yu saw her opportunity to rekindle her relationship with Lü Li. One afternoon, she appeared at his little office, which smelled of sweat, bearing a small bag of pork buns.

"I had extra," she said, "and I didn't want them to go

to waste."

Lü Li was just about to pick one up and take a bite when the phone on his desk rang. When he picked it up, the most extraordinary thing happened: he began to weep.

"Lü! My dear! What is it?" Ms Yu said. She put down the bag of buns and sat sideways on his desk, leaning towards him and reaching for his face. His eyeglasses were fogged, and his mouth gaped like a torn pants pocket. He stood up, pushed Ms Yu aside, and strode out of his office. She heard later from the other teachers that Lü Li's wife had been paralysed by a stroke.

Lü Li spent the better part of a month sleeping at the hospital next to his wife's bed, changing her IVs and her bedpans, rolling her onto a different side each night so that she would not get bedsores, and reading to her from the newspaper in case she could still understand, even if she could not express herself. At the end of the month, the doctor took Lü Li aside and told him there was nothing more they could do, that he could put her in a hospice, but the hospital was no longer the right place for her. Lü Li thanked him then went home to get the blue-metal tricycle truck. He bundled his wife in a heavy quilt and carried her to the bed of the truck, then he pedalled back to their apartment across from the stinking creek they call Liangmahe, river of the bright horses.

Lü Li, who was sixty that year, retired from the school and gave up the night watchman job. He spent his evenings at home, tenderly feeding his wife with the porridges and egg custards that he had prepared for her, soft things that she would not have to chew. He took her to the toilet and helped her up when she was done. He kept a damp towel on the back of his chair so that he could wipe her mouth.

Twice a week, he would fill a basin with warm water and wash her stringy grey hair, wrapping it in a towel-turban afterwards. Sometimes, while her hair dried, he would clip her toenails and massage lotion into her horny feet. His son argued that Lü Li should hire a caretaker for his mother; he said it would be better for the old lady and also better for Lü Li, who would surely deteriorate quickly now that he was constantly home with his mute wife. But Lü Li would not hear of allowing anyone else to care for his wife.

After a half year, she died. Lü Li had dozed off on the couch watching sports on TV. His wife had apparently got up by herself in the middle of the night to go to the bathroom, and she fell a few feet from the bed. He found her on the floor. She was wearing baggy underpants and a big cotton T-shirt with the Olympic rings on it and "Beijing Olympics 2008" written in English in a cheery blue script. She looked all crumpled on the floor, with her T-shirt hitched up to show a powdery roll of stomach flab. Lü Li straightened out her night clothes and rolled her onto her back, placing her hands over her stomach in what he viewed as a more dignified death pose, then he called the ambulance to take her away.

His son gave Lü Li the little dog Doudou, which became his treasured companion and recipient of many confidences.

"You know, I've never liked the school head," he would tell the dog as he fed him in the morning. "He's always been pompous, and he doesn't actually understand education."

"I can't go out to get fried dough sticks for breakfast," he said to Doudou as they were leaving for the morning walk. "That old man cheats me, and I don't have the heart to say anything."

Doudou looked up at him with adoring eyes. They trotted off together to the banks of the Liangmahe creek, and Lü Li let Doudou wander and graze while he sat on a stone bench. He waited for Mrs Wang to join them with her own Doudou. She and Lü Li would fall into conversation.

"They took my home and gave me a 'compensation unit' out in Pinggu," she told him one morning. "At first, I thought I was getting a good deal – it's much larger than the place I used to have. But it's just too far, and there's nothing around. Shopping is very inconvenient. So I'm staying with my son and daughter-in-law." She pointed in the direction of Lady Street, a new street that had opened up across from the Kempinski Hotel. "Over there."

"How is it, living with them?" asked Lü Li, politely.

"Awful." She unsnapped a pink plastic denture that held four realistic-looking teeth and took it out of her mouth to show Lü Li. "See this? I only wear it for meals – it's not very comfortable. I had it on the dinner table in its blue plastic box just the other night, and when I took it out to put into my mouth, my son acted as if I had farted at the table. 'Ma!' he said. 'You can't do that at the table! It's disgusting!' What does he expect of me? I don't like having fake teeth either, but I have to eat!"

"Living in your own house is always best."

"You can say that again. He doesn't like it if I wear shoes in the house for even a few minutes. Well, it takes me time to change into slippers! I need to sit down!"

"I know just how it is," Lü Li said.

The first night Mrs Wang stayed at his apartment, she lay down on the bed on her back fully clothed, with her arms at her sides like a soldier. Lü Li stayed in the living room. The next morning, she asked if he minded.

"I never stayed at a man's house before. My son will be scandalised."

"Let him," said Lü Li. "Just move your stuff in. You don't need to go back there anymore."

The next weekend, Mrs Wang had her son fill his car with her clothing, towels, quilt, a lamp, a small box of jewellery, an array of fragrant soaps, and the orthopedic pads that went in her shoes, and he moved her into the apartment Lü Li had shared with his wife. Every afternoon, Mrs Wang dusted the wife's photographs, and periodically, she would wash and press the dead woman's clothes and hang them back in the closet so they would smell fresh.

"She was a wonderful woman," Mrs Wang would tell the neighbours, though she had never met her. Eventually, Mrs Wang brought Doudou over to live with them, and this gave the humans in the house much amusement when they had to designate the dogs "Doudou 1" and "Doudou 2". The dogs, however, hated each other and tried to steal each other's food, such that Lü Li and Mrs Wang had to feed them in separate rooms with the doors closed.

One afternoon, Lü Li walked through the Kempinski department store just to see what was on sale. He took the escalators all the way to the fifth floor, where they sold crystal glasses and jade jewellery, and he was headed down the other side when he saw Nora peering at the jewellery cases. She was as slim and birdlike as she had been two years earlier, when he last saw her, and she was braced against the glass case with her fingers spread and bent over so her nose nearly touched the glass.

Lü Li turned away but just then, she must have looked up, because she called after him, "Lao Lü! It's me, Nora!" and reluctantly, he turned to look at her.

"I heard you retired," she said. Lü Li was surprised that she had inquired.

"I had to take care of my wife," he told her. "She had a stroke."

Nora knit her brows. "No! Really? I didn't hear about that. How is she now?"

"She's getting better. I take good care of her," Lü Li said. "I'm just getting her some bread from the bakery on the basement level. I don't know why I came up to this floor..."

"It's good of you to care for her as you do."

"She's a wonderful woman. I was very lucky to marry her," said Lü Li. He found he had nothing more to say to Nora. "Well, I have to get home."

"Maybe we can get together one weekend?" she said.

"I'm too busy. Take care."

C
O
C
K
R
O
A
C
H

Jia Yong, along with the other prospective employers, was walking up and down between wooden benches in a draughty room near Beijing's central train station, appraising girls who were lined up like so many bowling pins. It was a dank room below street level with cement walls and greasy light leaking in from casement windows that opened into cement wells built to allow for at least some light and air. The place smelled like some mixture of engine grease and cabbage. The girls appeared nervous and were all staring at their feet, but Jia Yong was preoccupied with trying to look like the kind of person who often comes to such an agency to hire staff, so he was not thinking about his specific needs or who might best fulfil them.

The girls, fresh in from dreary villages along the train

line to Beijing, had been instructed to stand and look down demurely when spoken to. Jia Yong stopped in front of one of these girls and inspected her. She jumped to her feet and looked at her toes, waiting for him to speak first, as the recruiter had instructed. Yong also looked at her shoes, thinking the girl must have dropped something that she was looking for. Hong'er glanced up with her head still bent, as if to prod him on, and Yong remembered that he was the one who should initiate the conversation.

"I'm looking for someone to care for my mother and my brother," he said. "They're disabled."

"I would love to care for them, Older Brother," she said, still looking down. The "Older Brother" was at once deferential and coquettish; Hong'er was twenty years Yong's junior and could have called him "Uncle". "Brother" made him feel closer and mysteriously powerful. "I also have a disabled father." This disability, although a spur-of-the-moment invention, was clearly an advantage for Hong'er. Yong was won over. He filled out the paperwork, paid the first month's wage to the agency through the barred window, and loaded Hong'er and her belongings onto the back of his tricycle cart.

Jia Yong had a Socialist Realist look, chiselled, like a Chinese Hardy Boy. He parted his hair on the side and wet the front to control a cowlick. He wore man-tailored shirts tucked into blue cloth pants. Everything about him bespoke earnestness, simplicity, and the absence of guile. Sitting in the blue metal cab of his tricycle cart with her clothes bundled into a pink-and-blue bag made of woven plastic, Hong'er considered that she could have done worse. "Your wife must be very busy and have no time to care for your mother," she said to his back at a traffic light.

"I have no wife," he said simply. "It's me, my mother, and my older brother." Hong'er considered this state of affairs and pitied Jia Yong but also saw opportunity.

Jia Yong had spent the majority of his forty-three years inside the one-bedroom apartment in Dongzhimen that he had shared with his parents and his older brother. The whole family, apart from Jia Yong himself, had been disabled. Shortly after Yong turned thirteen, his father had a stroke that paralysed him from the waist down. Since then, Jia Yong had cared for his parents and his brother.

Jia Yong was seen in the neighbourhood as a sort of holy fool. People made fun of the huge, slightly imbecilic smile he wore everywhere and of his willingness to provide any service, do any chore, usually at a run. Neighbours shook their heads at his personal simplicity, his humility, and the tenderness with which he cared for the family, qualities not generally seen in young men. He fed his rail-thin brother as one would a baby, pretending his hand was a crane and hoisting the soft gruel into Jia Wei's mouth. He took his mother on weekend excursions to botanical gardens, though she had to be diapered because of her ruined kidneys and pushed in a wheelchair so that she wouldn't tire too much. "You're in charge while I'm gone, Brother!" he would call over his shoulder to his brother, slumped in a corner, as he trundled his mother out the door on a Saturday. Jia Yong had a few vices that no one took very seriously. He loved to gamble and had a weekly poker night with a group of neighbourhood ne'er-do-wells who regularly won money off him. He had a longstanding relationship with a married woman whose husband mistreated her.

Since Jia Yong's teenage years, the family had lived

mostly off the rough charity of the local Street Committee. The Jias considered themselves a collective burden and were grateful to the state for its care, which the family viewed as discretionary and therefore benevolent. The toothpaste factory allocated a small apartment to the family in the Dongzhimen neighbourhood, then a semi-rural area at the eastern edge of the city. Jia Yong proposed that his mother occupy the single small bedroom at the front of the apartment, but Bai Lingru wanted to sleep next to her older son lest he need her in the night. Their living arrangements were managed jointly by the now-bankrupt toothpaste factory that had once employed Jia Yong's parents and the Street Committee that watched over their low-rise apartment complex. The factory had given them the apartment without compensation – at the time, there was no market for the apartments anyway. But the factory management – still in place though the factory had stopped production years earlier – considered that its responsibilities towards the family ended there.

The Street Committee was to provide ongoing support. It decided that a small lean-to in the yard of the apartment complex could be used as a little store, and they bestowed rights to the space on the Jias. From the age of sixteen, Jia Yong managed the shop, renting it to a succession of entrepreneurs from the south, who sold clothing and knick-knacks with varying levels of success or failure. Over the last few years, the current operator was a Sichuanese businessman named Nie who sold children's clothes and paid Jia Yong some rent – far less than it was worth but more than Jia Yong ever expected to receive. The local government also gave the Jia family a stipend.

After Jia Yong's father had suffered a second stroke

in 1995 – over twenty years earlier – Jia Yong had been freed to find work. He felt he could do better for the family by hiring a country girl to care for his mother and brother and himself going out to work. He calculated that he could pay a live-in housemaid three hundred a month and himself make seven hundred as a bicycle messenger, a job he held until 1999. Then he found higher-paying work as a prep cook, a job he still held. The rental income, the stipend, and Jia Yong's wage were enough for him to feed the family and pay a housemaid.

But the volume and grimness of the work in the Jia household compared unfavourably with the rate Jia Yong was willing to pay. His brother, Jia Wei, needed a good deal of care. He suffered from seizures, sometimes several a day. He could communicate only through awkward vocalisations that his brother and mother understood as happiness, hunger, pain, just as new parents interpret their babies' cries, but that outsiders heard only as annoying yelps. Jia Wei needed to be fed, dressed, and taken to the toilet, tasks that the young women working as housekeepers tended to find distasteful in a middle-aged man, no matter what his disability.

Consequently, Jia Yong frequently lost these young women to the heavy workload and ordinary pay; wages were rising quickly then, and Jia Yong refused to recognise this reality, grudgingly adding an extra fifty each time the recruitment agencies told him he was paying too little to find anyone.

Care for the family had meant that Jia Yong's world was limited to this apartment, with its flaking whitewashed walls and cement floor. The sole privilege Jia Yong claimed was to take the front bedroom as his own. The bedroom was the only room in the apartment with a door that closed; his mother and brother both slept in the living room, where a curtain separated his brother's, bed from his mother's twin bed. For meals, the family pulled a folding table out from under the mother's bed. When the old man was still alive, Jia Yong would prop him up on two pillows and turn his father's head towards the table as if to play act someone who was involved in the dinner-table conversation.

Jia Yong slept in a steel-frame single bed with a heavy cotton quilt that he rolled into a tight coil every morning and placed at the foot of the bed, military style. The room's sole adornment was Jia Yong's calendar from 2010, which showed a fat baby wearing a strong-man singlet and smiling maniacally as he held up a ripe peach with both hands, as if it were a prize he had won in an Olympic event. The room had a narrow double window with lead-framed panes that opened with a crank onto the front courtyard. Jia Yong kept a curtain pulled across the window at all times, since the apartment was on the first floor.

Jia Yong's apartment was a disadvantage when hiring live-in help. The complex had been built in the late 1980s but looked much older. It comprised five buildings of five stories each, with three units on each floor. The entrances were dark and cold, with a layer of greasy dust coating the railings and the mailboxes on the first floor of each building. Just inside the Jia family's entrance, bicycles leaned layers deep against the walls and looked like they had not been used in years. A bell-shaped birdcage perched on top of the seats of three bicycles leaning one against the other, and right outside Jia's front door were two cardboard boxes that had once held a desktop computer, along with an oily rag on top of the monitor box. The entryway smelled of something rank and cold, like a cavern frequented by bats.

Jia Yong parked the bicycle cart outside the door and picked up Hong'er's bundle. They stepped into the shade of the building entrance, and it immediately became cooler. The building smelled like damp stone, like being in a cave. They walked up three small steps, and Jia Yong opened the door on the left side of the landing to an odour of urine mingled with the kerosene that Jia Yong periodically used to mop the floors. The apartment was arranged like a barbell, with Jia Yong's small bedroom in front, a narrow hall that opened onto the kitchen on one side and bathroom on the other, and common room in back separated from the hall with a slatted rubber curtain.

Bai Lingru had been sitting close to her older son, cracking sunflower seeds with her teeth and feeding him the tiny kernel inside. She looked up at Jia Yong and Hong'er.

"Her hands are too small," the old lady observed to no one in particular.

"Auntie, I am happy to meet you," said Hong'er, briefly bending in an awkward approximation of a curtsey. "And this is Mr Jia's handsome older brother?" She ran a hand over the back of Jia Wei's head. Jia Wei leaned his head back, his hands in his lap, and squeezed a sound out of his twisted mouth. "Ahh-yee."

"He is calling me Ayi," Hong'er exclaimed. "No," she said to Jia Wei, leaning close to his face, "you call me by my name, Little Hong. I must call you Older Brother, and Mr Jia Yong will be Second Brother."

Bai Lingru was watching the proceedings. She felt a surge of tenderness for her older boy – now in his early forties – and simultaneous hostility for this new housekeeper. But she said nothing. She knew that Jia Yong was already heavily burdened with care for her and Jia Wei, and she did not want to make things worse. Besides, if the previous girls were anything to go by, this one would last only a few weeks.

"You have small feet," she said to Hong'er. Hong'er looked down at the white Feiyue sneakers with rounded rubber toes that made her diminutive feet look even smaller.

"I guess you are right, Auntie."

"Small feet, small heart," the old lady said quietly. She looked off to the side and repeated the phrase three more times.

"Come on," said Jia Yong, leading Hong'er away. "She's not right in the head," but the old woman, narrowing her eyes, watched Hong'er. Hong'er hawked loudly and spit a glob of mucus into the garbage pail in the kitchen.

Jia Yong had obtained a single bed and placed it next to the couch where his brother slept so that Hong'er could be there to administer to him at night. Jia Yong felt guilty about keeping his room with the closed door but told himself that Hong'er must be used to poor conditions since she came from the countryside.

"You have a lot of light here, Brother," she commented. "This bed will do nicely."

Hong'er was aware that, at the beginning at least, she would occupy the most subservient position in the household, rising earliest and going to bed latest, accepting criticism without complaint, eating leftovers, carrying heavy loads, acting extra grateful if brought along on any excursion.

She trailed around after Jia Yong, who showed her the sun porch, where there were stacked empty boxes and broken whisks, dry gourds, old newspapers, and anything else he picked up from the street and thought to save. They walked back through the apartment, and he opened the door to his room. "That's my bedroom," he said. Hong'er said nothing, standing with her arms crossed.

Hong'er slept in the day room for just two weeks before Jia Yong's guilt got the better of him.

"How are you doing here?" he asked her one evening.

"You are very kind to me," she said. "It is hard to get any sleep next to your brother."

Jia Yong shifted. "It's pretty crowded in there, isn't it?"

"I understand. You don't have space to spare. I go into the bathroom when I need to change my clothes."

Jia Yong had forgotten that a young woman might feel modest around his older brother. He was so accustomed to bathing and toileting Jia Wei that he did not really think of him as a man.

Jia Yong moved his bedroll into the day room, next to the sofa where his brother slept. Hong'er moved her parcels to the bedroom, placed the zippered bag on the bed, unzipped the top, and began putting her things away. By the time Jia Yong came back into the room, she had placed a hairbrush and a small tube of rose-scented hand cream on the dresser, and the faint floral odour wafted into the air. She began to spend a good bit of time in that room with the door closed.

"She listens to music all day," Bai Lingru told her son when he got home from work.

"Ma, she's a young girl. She needs entertainment. Not like you and me."

Bai Lingru could see her son growing fascinated with this stubby country girl who had such self-confidence, and she saw that Hong'er enjoyed the attention. *It's not like my generation*, thought Bai Lingru. *We never would have presumed to be on the same level. Yong is too kind-hearted.*

Bai Lingru had never been among the entitled, the people who are politely greeted in restaurants, who fit the clothes in the store, who look like they may buy the products on offer. She had always assumed a supporting role in other people's lives. But now, as she aged, she found she had to assert her presence more, because she needed help. She could not walk far without an arm to lean on. Her weak kidneys meant she had to stay close to a toilet, because she could not hold for more than about forty minutes. Her eyesight was failing, and the streets looked dark to her. So she became more and more reliant on her son and more fearful of being alone.

Bai Lingru was scatterbrained. Left to her own devices, she would turn on the stove and forget about it or eat mouldy rice from a pot that had been left on the counter. The only medically identifiable problem she had was her weak kidneys, but perhaps by virtue of having shared a room for many years with a husband and son who could not communicate verbally, she had an unworldly approach to conversation. She maintained a dialogue with invisible presences in the apartment, including late at night, when she would wake up alone, turn on a light, and conduct a quiet conversation with someone no one else could see.

Hong'er had arrived in Beijing as so many country girls did, seeking prospects that she did not have at home. She had grown up outside of Hengshui, one of the miserable industrial cities in southern Hebei Province that had never bothered to develop, since Beijing was just three hours away. Even in its downtown area, Hengshui was unrelentingly practical, with no parks, no shrubbery along its avenues, not even any ornamentation on the streetlamps. Its most famous industry was snuff bottles, painted from the inside, for which distinction the city made sure to employ children under twelve, whose little hands could fit into the necks of the bottles. Since the Hengshui city fathers did not want to break any child labour laws, they ordered primary school art classes to teach classes in "interior painting" and provided them with the bottles and the model designs and paid them a subsidy. From when she was seven to twelve, Hong'er had painted these bottles in her school. She could have got a job at the local arts and crafts factory, but by the time she got out of junior high, she was fed up with bottles and wanted to see the wider world.

Like all such cities, Hengshui had a development zone with unoccupied high-rises and strips of empty shops to which the developer had assigned names that evoked without infringing upon the names of famous foreign establishments: Stanbucks, Adipas, Guzzi. Hong'er's family lived in a village abutting the development zone where there was absolutely nothing to do except watch the TV soaps about heroic but crusty old army officers and young people who got rich too quickly and lost interest in their spouses. She sat with her parents in the dim living room in the evening in front of the glowing television and dreamed of living in one of the big cities in the soaps, someplace like Shenzhen.

Her parents farmed barley, and Hong'er worked alongside them and her older brother pending such time as she could meet an eligible young man, marry, and move out. Her potential wedding was a matter of constant discussion and voluble anxiety on the part of her mother, who coldly appraised the negotiable gifts that her daughter could offer and found them wanting. Hong'er was small-statured and inclined to plumpness, with stubby fingers, a snub nose, and thin, oily hair. The hair was unevenly cut at the shoulder and incongruously clipped at the dome of her head with a pin that bore a blue plastic hat at a jaunty tilt, recalling a small donkey wearing a straw hat on one ear. Hong'er's had an air of sly self-consciousness that suggested insolence.

Like many of the young people in that part of suburban Hengshui, Hong'er had been unable to pass the exams for high school and had attended only junior high. Her intellectual gifts were ordinary, and her family could not afford the prep classes that nearly every student who passed the exam took. Without an education or money to offer an eligible young man, her family could provide no hope of social advancement to a potential son-in-law. Hong'er's mother worried that her daughter would be passed over and reach her twenties with no proposals, putting her market value on a rapid trajectory, like unsold food, to decline, so that any presentable young man would be well advised to wait for Hong'er's price to depreciate. About these concerns, her mother spoke frequently and at a length propelled by high anxiety, causing her daughter to take the opposite point of view as antidote to her mother's nagging.

Hong'er's father said little and avoided being drawn into the marriage discussions, which he considered the realm of women and a topic best left without masculine comment. Hong'er's mother often pushed him to take her side, but the old man would grunt and leave for the fields or, in the evening, turn to the newscast on television.

Hong'er felt, under the circumstances, that Hengshui held no future for her. She was disinclined to hang around waiting for the man who might or might not appear, and she was annoyed by her mother's nagging. Hong'er had carried on an affair for over a year with a chicken farmer who lived in the same village, who was thirty-five, married, and had an eight-year-old son. Marriage was out of the question, but the affair tended to blunt Hong'er's interest in the mangy boys who were eligible. She decided to make a move. Hengshui had a labour agency that placed young women as domestics in Beijing, so one afternoon, without telling her parents, Hong'er made her way downtown and found a recruitment agent.

"What sort of position are you looking for?" the recruiter asked.

"I want to work in someone's home. It's safer that way. You have a family to care for you." Hong'er had a schoolfriend who had gone to Beijing as a domestic and advised her to give this answer. The other jobs that offered room and board – as a server in a restaurant or working in a foot-massage parlour – had hidden risks of getting lured into the sex trade. "You may end up with a hateful family," said her friend, "but at least you'll be safe living in your employer's home, and you can always ask the agency to reassign you."

Hong'er tended to invite sympathy from men and exasperation from women. She had large, pleading eyes under a blunt fringe and short fingers that clutched at her sleeves. Her heart-shaped face was sallow and unremarkable, but the manner in which she stole glances up from a downcast face suggested coquettishness within deep humility, a combination that a certain type of man found fetching. Hong'er was diminutive in her white sneakers and yet had ropy arms and a mule's back; she could have loaded steel girders onto trucks for a living. The weakness and vulnerability she displayed were a semaphore of femininity, like wearing high-heeled shoes to a job as a grocery clerk.

Jia Yong's move into the main room meant that he was able to get up at night and help his brother urinate, so Hong'er could sleep through the night. Each morning, she rose at seven and put on a pot to make a thin gruel from the rice left over from dinner. While it was boiling, Jia Yong helped his older brother with toileting and bathing. His mother opened up a card table and arranged two stools by her older son's bed for the morning meal. Jia Yong would sit with Jia Wei and feed him his porridge. Sometimes, they had eggs.

After clearing up the breakfast dishes and sweeping the floor, Hong'er took a walk, often lingering in the courtyard of the Jias's apartment complex, and there she made friends with Nie, the proprietor of the small shop selling children's clothing who paid rent to the Jia family. Nie had closed the shop off from the sidewalk with a slatted plastic curtain and lined the inside walls with pink-

and blue-striped plastic that came from the cheap bags that migrants used to carry the knick-knacks they were planning to sell at market. He strung wires horizontally across the walls of the shop four high then hung up the little sweatpants and sweatshirts from the wires with dirty plastic clothes hangers. Jia Yong never saw any customers there and wondered how Nie made enough to pay his rent, but he was glad of the income and didn't inquire. Hong'er would help him find the right size when a customer came in looking for a small sweatshirt or winter jacket, allowing Nie to keep his eyes on the customer and make sure nothing was stolen. She got along well with Nie, an ex-convict who had churned through all sorts of menial jobs, including selling shish kebab on the street and cleaning at the German School. None of these pursuits brought in much money, and Nie felt that he was destined for greater things.

"I wonder if you'd like to earn some extra money," he said to her one morning. She had invested only three weeks in getting to know him.

"I'd love to," she replied.

"I can get T-shirts much more cheaply in Sichuan than here in Beijing. I need someone to travel to Sichuan to pick them up. I have a friend who will get them for me, and I'll buy the train ticket. All you have to do is ride the train to Chengdu, pick up the package at my friend's apartment, and bring it back to me, and I'll pay you two thousand. It will take you two days."

Hong'er was stunned by the lofty payment offered. "Why don't you go yourself and save the money?" she said.

"I don't have the time. I have to mind the store."

"You can't have them sent?"

"Delivery is very unreliable."

Hong'er felt there was something wrong with the arrangement but was happy enough to go along with Nie's explanation. Two thousand for two days' work.

"I have to ask the Jias if they'll give me the time off."

"Tell them they can dock your salary by two hundred renminbi. And tell them you earn one thousand a trip. You don't want them to be jealous."

The two hundred she had them knock off her salary was enough to preserve Jia Yong's pride, so that he did not feel he was being taken advantage of. And even after the two hundred, the eighteen hundred net that Hong'er earned was an unimaginably high sum for two days of riding a train. From then on, she made one, sometimes two trips per month. Her main contact, whom she called Older Brother, was a rough man with a shaved head and a tattoo on the back of his neck, who wore tight-fitting black T-shirts, precisely the sort of person Hong'er would have called a criminal, a mafia member, if she had just seen him on the street. By her second trip, she had come to realise that she was not just carrying T-shirts to Beijing. Older Brother warned her not to look into the satchel she carried, a low-quality white, blue, and pink woven bag of the sort that thousands of people from the countryside carried. Hong'er was happy enough to oblige: she wanted deniability in case something illegal was in the bag.

All the extra money from the Sichuan trips made Hong'er feel rich, and she began to make small improvements to the apartment. She bought a colourful space rug for her bedroom. She pasted decals of bright-red lips to the frosted glass on the bathroom door. After one run, Nie gave her a bonus, and, feeling magnanimous, Hong'er bought a bucket of pale-purple paint and suggested to Jia Yong that he spend the weekend brightening up the place. By Monday, the whole apartment was lavender. Hong'er congratulated herself on bringing the Jia family into the modern era.

"Auntie, why don't we get a rug?" she said to Jia Yong's mother, as they sat drinking tea after Hong'er's morning walk. "I can go to the market and find something nice that will complement the purple walls."

Jia Yong's mother looked up at her. She had a long, bony face with skin the colour of a rubber band and the same sense of elasticity.

"The floor is there to serve people," she said. "When a rug comes into the house, people serve the floor."

"You're so old-fashioned, Auntie," Hong'er said, but she let it go. Two days later, she bought a small orange rug with a long shag.

Hong'er turned out to be the most indolent of the housekeepers Jia Yong had hired. She refused to toilet or bathe Jia Wei on the grounds that it was improper for a young woman, so Jia Yong handled the more intimate tasks. He also found himself mopping the floor and washing the clothes, because when he pointed out to Hong'er tasks that needed to be done, she cheerfully acknowledged the comments, but her memory seemed as transient as the flickerings of the television late at night.

"I don't like her," said his mother when Hong'er was in the bathroom showering. "She does not have a good heart."

"Ma, you know how hard it's been to keep anyone."

When Jia Yong was home, Hong'er lavished attention on his mother, slicing fruit for her, rushing to take her arm when the old lady stood, offering to take her for walks. But once left on her own, she would bark at the old lady to stay in her chair.

"I don't want to sit," the old lady said.

"Then walk around if you like, but don't expect me to help if you fall down."

The old lady puttered around the apartment, peering with exaggerated care at the potted plants and going out onto the dusty, glassed-in porch at the back of the apartment to take drying clothes down from their plastic clothespins. After that, not being able to think of another activity, she went to sit in the wide, wooden chair with flowered tied-on pillows that was unofficially hers.

"I'd like a cup of tea," Bai Lingru said to Hong'er, who poured cold jasmine tea from the pot into the Nescafé jar that she used for drinking. Bai Lingru set the jar on the arm of her chair and picked up the remote to turn on the TV. In doing so, she jostled the bottle, which pitched off the armchair and onto the floor, splintering into tiny shards of glass. Hong'er strode over and backhanded the old woman hard across the face, leaving a livid strawberry mark.

"If you just did what I told you, you'd be safe in your chair. Now you've gone and broken your jar, and I have to clean it up. And I'm not going to be able to find you a new one."

For Bai Lingru, the slap simply confirmed what she already knew about Hong'er: she was an evil, calculating girl with one face for Jia Yong and another for when he was gone.

The girl was particularly rough with Jia Wei, whom she viewed as barely sentient, and would push him into his chair and cuff him across the ears if he moved too slowly. He grew very thin, as Hong'er lacked the patience to sit with him as he slurped his food, so she would whisk away the bowl at the smallest provocation. "If you're going to slop your food on the floor," she told him," you just won't eat." Once, Bai Lingru seized Hong'er's arm as she raised it to strike Jia Wei. Hong'er spun around, shook the old lady loose, and struck the side of her head so hard that her left ear rung for an hour.

It had been four months, and Hong'er did not seem to be going anywhere. Bai Lingru stepped up her campaign to get her son to send Hong'er home.

"I think her parents need her to help with the harvest," she whispered to Jia Yong when Hong'er was in her bedroom.

"Ma, what are you talking about?"

Bai Lingru's pupils skittered furtively across the opening between her eyelids. Her eyes had a dimmed, milky cast from cataracts. Jia Yong made a mental note to take her to the eye doctor.

Hong'er started to slap and kick the old woman with some frequency. The disabled brother could not tell Jia Yong, and his mother said nothing, because she knew she would be alone with Hong'er the next day. Hong'er herself was secure in the knowledge that the old lady was given to fantasies, so it would be her word against Hong'er's, and Hong'er was the more persuasive liar.

So old Bai Lingru kept her peace and covertly continued the campaign to persuade her son to fire Hong'er and send her back to Hebei.

Hong'er settled on the idea of locking up the old lady and her son in order to leave the apartment during the day to sit and chat with Nie in his clothing stall. One weekday, Jia Yong came home early from work and found his mother and brother locked in the tiny bathroom and Hong'er nowhere to be found. She had secured the aluminium handle to a hook on the wall using a bicycle lock. The old lady stood straddling the reeking squat toilet, and Jia Wei crouched with his back against the wall, holding his head in his hands. Yong released them both, installed his brother on the couch with a cup of hot tea, and sat massaging his mother's feet. Hong'er returned.

"Where did you go this afternoon?" Jia Yong asked. "You should be caring for my family, not going out during the day. I waited nearly two hours for you."

"I had to go shopping, Brother Yong," she said, "and I got lost. I don't know my way around Beijing."

Hong'er had not brought back any groceries. She looked down, again summoned tears, and inched closer to Jia Yong. "Brother Yong, being close to you has made me so happy. I don't want to leave you."

They were standing in the front bedroom. The room smelled faintly of Hong'er's rose-scented hand cream. Hong'er had drawn so close that Jia Yong could hear her exhalations. She looked up at him. Jia Yong was much the taller. She began to undress him. Something about the self-assurance contained within this diminutive frame caused Jia Yong's thoughts to puddle and slop one into another. His eyes went liquid. Soon he found himself in bed with Hong'er. She assured him that she was taking the pill.

"Why would you need that?" he asked.

"It makes my periods more regular and keeps me from

getting cramps." This sounded entirely plausible to Jia Yong, who put the question out of his mind.

Hong'er determined that she would make her life in Beijing, and she set her sights on marrying Jia Yong as the nearest path to gaining a residence permit for the city. Although Jia Yong was in his forties, Hong'er felt that he had the character of a boy of twelve or thirteen and could be easily controlled.

If it were not for the expensively dressed but rough-looking men who came to their apartment to pick up the semi-monthly package and hand over money each time Hong'er returned, Jia Yong would have been able to maintain a certain indeterminacy around the transaction, holding open the possibility that Hong'er was engaged in some kind of international trade. But the air of violence that surrounded these men made the hair on the back of his neck stand up. He could not say exactly why. They dressed better than the men in Jia Yong's neighbourhood, in colourful golf shirts instead of T-shirts with slogans, and wore tasselled loafers and trousers with a sharp crease. Their watches were expensive. Jia Yong would persuade them to sit as he fluttered around pulling beers out of the refrigerator and setting out a dish of peanuts, but they paid him no mind. He imagined that, despite a half dozen meetings of this kind, they did not know his name. He understood, as they did, that the money they were bringing purchased his obsequiousness.

Winter turned to spring, and Hong'er became pregnant.

"I should never have bought the pills at an outdoor market," she told Jia Yong. In reality, she had stopped taking them almost as soon as their sexual relationship had begun. "But I suppose we should marry. Otherwise it will be too late for you to have a child, and for your mother to see her grandchild."

Jia Yong, surprisingly, was reluctant. "I have to take care of my family," he said. "I don't have time for a family of my own. What would Wei do if I abandoned him?"

"There are institutions."

"Those are terrible places. You wouldn't put your father in one of those places, would you?" Yong remembered that Hong'er's father was disabled.

"Why would I do that? He's not that old." She had forgotten about her father's disability. Yong interpreted this, however, as filial care.

"That is the way I feel about my brother. I cannot marry as long as I have him to take care of."

Hong'er got an abortion, but she chose to ignore Jia Yong's comment about marrying. Jia Yong had her stay in bed for a week after the abortion, and he made her soups and custards. After that, Hong'er resumed her duties as a housemaid. She decided she needed to be more strategic about marriage.

"Brother Yong, why don't we have wedding pictures taken? It doesn't mean that we have to marry, but I would like to send some beautiful pictures to my parents so that they won't worry about me. I'll pay for them."

"Why would we do that? Everyone will think we are married."

Hong'er's eyes teared up. "You are a man and you don't understand the pressure I'm under. My parents have arranged for me to marry, and they insist that I go back to Hengshui. He is an old man with children. I don't want to go." As she said it, the story became almost real in Hong'er's mind. Jia Yong would have been a beast not to consent.

Hong'er found a studio, and they spent eight hundred to have wedding photos taken. They selected a variety of costumes: a powder-blue gown with puffy sleeves for Hong'er and a purple shirt and yellow tie for Jia Yong in the "engagement" sequence, in front of a backdrop of the Eiffel Tower, and a white wedding dress for Hong'er and morning coat for Jia Yong for the "wedding". A week later, Jia Yong picked up the photos. There was a large, framed portrait of himself in the morning coat and a grey ascot standing behind Hong'er's shoulder as she sat, hands in her lap and half smile on her face, on a settee, folds of white crepe arranged across her knees like whitecaps on a rough ocean. There was an outsized album with enamelled covers, holding twenty-four photographs with different themes – Jia Yong and Hong'er leaning against a Rolls Royce. Jia Yong and Hong'er holding hands and looking into each other's eyes before backdrops of Big Ben, the Egyptian Sphinx, the Grand Canyon. Jia Yong smoking and looking sidelong, knowingly, into the camera. Hong'er standing on a little plot of grass, with the blue sky in the background furnished by Photoshop.

Although he knew the photos were merely to allay her parents' worries about Hong'er, Jia Yong began thinking of her differently. Chopping carrots in the restaurant, his mind wandered to Hong'er's small feet in their flat-soled sneakers and to the odd bow legs encased in her jeans with pink embroidery on the back pocket. He held her image in his mind all day, and yet when he got home and saw the real Hong'er, his breath caught at the reality of her. She seemed more competent, more independent than Jia Yong. He worried about losing her. He did not object when she placed the photo of the two of them in wedding

167

outfits leaning against the Rolls Royce on a shelf over the television set, where visitors could all see and remark upon it. Nothing else changed. No one said any more about the photographs. All of them continued exactly as in the past.

Except that, when Hong'er made her twice-monthly run to Sichuan, Jia Yong saw her off at the station and met her on her return. The trips seemed to lift her spirits, and after she got back, the men wearing golf shirts and expensive watches would come to the Jia family's apartment to pick up the package that Hong'er had brought and hand her a thick packet of money to carry back. Jia Yong never looked inside Hong'er's bag. Without fully understanding what she was doing, he knew that he'd best remain a bystander. He marvelled at Hong'er's calm and, in fact, high spirits in this work. It seemed that Hong'er had a comfort with this segment of society that could only have come from proximity. She seemed to come alive when the Beijing contacts came over to pick up the package of drugs. She smiled and joked with them, made them sit down and drink a beer, knew just how familiar to be without losing a sense of deference.

Bai Lingru gave up hope that her son would send the girl home. She hoped only that he would not marry her.

One summer evening, Jia Yong returned home around midnight to find his brother curled on one side on his bed, moaning. "What's wrong with him?" he asked Hong'er.

"Just a flu, I guess. He'll get over it."

"But he was fine when I left this morning."

"Flu can be really fast," she said.

Jia Yong held a pail for Jia Wei as he vomited repeatedly. By 2 a.m., Jia Wei's skin was clammy, and his eyes were rolling up into his head.

"You need to take him to the hospital," his mother said. She was hovering over Jia Wei with a damp towel, which she placed on his forehead then took to rinse and wet again. Jia Yong carried Jia Wei to the tricycle truck, tucked him in with a heavy quilt, and pedalled hard for the hospital in Jingguang. The trip took about twenty minutes.

Jia Wei lasted the night. The hospital pumped the contents of his stomach into a large enamel basin. Jia Yong sat in the hall holding his brother's hand. Jia Wei was still on a gurney in the corridor, as the doctor felt it would be a waste of resources to admit him. Around three in the morning, a young doctor wearing a white cloth cap came up to Jia Yong. "I'm afraid the sepsis was too far gone. Your brother's blood pressure is dropping very quickly. In these situations, we don't have much hope."

"Sepsis?"

"That's when you have an infection that isn't treated properly, and it gets into your bloodstream."

Jia Yong was confused, as his brother had never had an infection left untreated, but he thought the term "sepsis" might be more broadly applied. Jia Wei was sweating, and his limbs trembled. The way he was groaning and turning his head back and forth made it clear he felt deeply nauseous.

The perfunctory cremation at Babaoshan, without even Jia Wei's mother in attendance, was even more forlorn than his brother's life had been. Since Jia Wei had rarely left the house, there were no friends or classmates to attend. A squat, unsmiling woman sold Jia Yong a small paper wreath with "Rest in Peace" lettered on a paper banner across the front, and a young woman whose card said she worked in "promotions" for the crematorium asked whether he wanted to pay 100 renminbi to have Chopin's funeral march played in the cremation room. Yong paid and solemnly listened. He placed the paper wreath on top of his brother's body as it was rolled into the oven. He was told he could keep the ashes if he paid 500 renminbi for the carrying box; he declined. Then he took the long subway ride home.

"Ma!" he said by way of greeting. His mother was sitting on a small stool facing the bare wall in the main room.

"It's all because of that girl that he has to crawl around on the floor," Jia Yong's mother muttered. She pried open a sunflower seed with her teeth. She cracked it with her fingernails, sucked out the kernel, then slipped the dried white-and-black striped shell into her mouth, licked off the salt, and spit out the two halves of shell onto a small, damp pile on the floor.

"Who has to crawl around?"

"Wei. Scurrying around in the dirt, anyone could step on him. Look, there he is!"

Jia Yong went over to see what his mother was pointing at. It was a slender brown cockroach scurrying along the seam between wall and floor.

Jia Yong went to sit with his mother.

"He was a kind person," she said.

"He was," said Jia Yong, stroking her arm.

"People think having a son like that is a burden, or maybe not really like having a son at all. They would always ask about you and get embarrassed if I talked about Jia Wei too. But it's the heart, not the mind. Wei was kind. Wei was good."

This may have been more words than Jia Yong had ever heard his mother put together into contiguous sentences. He cried and tried to hide the tears.

Bai Lingru captured the roach and kept it in a jar with air holes punched in the lid. Sometimes, she released it onto the wall, saying it needed exercise.

Days passed and yet the old woman did not give up the idea that Jia Wei was a cockroach. Mostly, she mumbled indistinctly. When she and Hong'er were alone, she said nothing about the cockroach, but when Jia Yong was there, she spoke loudly.

"Look! There he is climbing up the wall!" she said one evening, as they watched a soccer match on TV. "Poor Wei! Who made him a cockroach?"

Hong'er ignored the old woman. Her eyes followed Jia Yong, catlike, with proprietary satisfaction. He felt embarrassed for his mother, something that would not have happened before Hong'er.

"Yong, get your mother her cigarettes. She wants to smoke." Post wedding photos, she no longer called him Older Brother. Jia Yong's mother noted the difference, dissatisfied.

Jia Yong fetched the cigarettes then returned to the main room. Hong'er slipped behind him and drew close, so that her nose almost grazed the cloth of his shirt. Jia Yong moved forward very slightly, enough to suggest discomfort, not enough to expunge his sense of ambivalence. Hong'er moved forward and whispered between his shoulder blades.

"Why don't we take a little nap together."

He tightened but did not say anything.

"Your mother won't even notice. We'll say we're

going out to buy some onions."

"Don't be ridiculous." He shrugged her off.

That evening, Jia Yong cooked a simple dinner. He rinsed the rice bowls, and swept the floor. Hong'er put the back of her hand to her forehead.

"I think I have a bit of a fever," she said to the room at large. "Yong, would you mind if I lie down in the bedroom?" She flung the smallest possible smile at Yong. He followed her into the bedroom.

"Let me feel your head," Jia Yong said, as Hong'er lay down on the single bed in the front room.

"It's a very low fever," she said. "Feel with your forehead."

He leaned forward and pressed his forehead to hers. She kept her eyes open and smiled at him. She opened her blouse and pulled his hands inside, where it was warm. She was wearing only a satin undershirt with skinny straps, and it was over her head in a moment so that he could touch the teacup breasts. She was slightly plump, undelineated, with little indentation for the waist, but her skin felt soft beneath his hands, inviting. He grabbed hold at either side of her waist, a fistful of warm skin. She undid his trousers. He collapsed afterward on top of her and fell asleep. Breathing underneath him, Hong'er triumphed in this little bit of carelessness – Jia Yong was normally so careful of the sensibilities of others, so solicitous of their comfort, that she interpreted placing his heavier frame onto hers as a mark of trust.

Weeks later, Jia Yong could not stop looking at his brother's empty bed or stop expecting to hear him call out when he returned from work in the evening. For Hong'er, all trace of Jia Wei was forgotten. She sang as she cleaned up around the apartment.

"See, there he is!" said Jia Yong's mother. "Back here to see us." She stood and cupped her hand over the cockroach that was scaling the whitewashed wall. "Look, Yong! Your brother has come to visit!"

Bai Lingru settled onto her small stool and rocked back and forth. "Pour me some tea, Yongyong."

By this time, Jia Yong had found her a replacement for the Nescafé jar. He went over, and she leaned up to whisper in his ear. She said just above a whisper, "She fed him poison. I know, because she always refused to feed him. That day she said to me, 'Ma, I'll feed Wei today. You go lie down.' I never should have let her do it. She put poison in his food. His stomach started to hurt, he was in such pain, and he died."

"Ma! Go to bed!"

Jia Yong got his mother settled for the night and went into the bedroom with Hong'er, who was already sitting on their narrow bed wearing a yellow slip. Jia Yong dawdled taking off his street clothes.

"What's the matter? Don't you love me? Don't you want to come share my bed?"

He stretched out on his back next to her.

"Of course I do. I'm just tired. Can we just sleep tonight?"

"I knew you didn't really love me!" Hong'er used her poutiest voice, but, getting no reaction, she rolled over and went to sleep.

Jia Yong dreamed that he was eating dry white powder, like the boric acid used to kill cockroaches, by the handful, pushing it into his mouth with a flat-backed trowel of some kind and choking it down even as he cried and begged – whom? – to let him stop and to give him something to drink. He woke with tears running down his cheeks. He got up to get some water from the thermos in the kitchen. Shuffling in his flimsy white slippers, taken from a hotel years before, he tried to keep from waking his mother. But he saw that she was sitting in the orange glow of the television set, watching a variety programme.

Still staring at the TV, she was talking quietly, to herself or maybe for Jia Yong's benefit. "People hate you now. They think you're a pest, crawling all over. Poor thing, you have to come out for food at night, or people will crush you! Don't worry, your mother will feed you."

"Ma, are you talking to Wei?"

"You go ahead up the wall! I'll be there when you come down."

"Ma, you know he's gone."

She turned to him in what seemed to be a moment of clarity. "What's the harm? Maybe Wei is really there."

"Ma, you said Hong'er killed him. We can't talk like that. Suppose the neighbours don't understand that there's something wrong with your thinking? Suppose they believe you?"

"But maybe I'm right." She kept looking at the television.

In a moment of horrifying clarity, Jia Yong realised his mother probably was right. Hong'er had murdered his brother.

He filled his tin enamel cup from the thermos and returned to the bedroom. Hong'er was sleeping rolled in the quilt that they shared. Jia Yong pried a section of the quilt from under her body and slipped in next to her so that he could feel the warmth of her body in its polyester slip. Hong'er hardly wore anything to bed, a habit Jia Yong found impossibly exotic. Every other girl he'd been with – in fact, everyone he had ever known – wore long johns to bed, as was sensible in the Beijing winter. He put an arm over her plump shoulders, which were rising and falling softly, and he went to sleep.

In the past, they had set up the small folding table next to Jia Wei's bed for the evening meal and taken it down when they cleaned up for more space. At meals, Jia Wei would lean against the wall, his hands twisted up at the wrist, while Jia Yong sat next to him and fed him. Now, Jia Yong could not bear to get rid of his brother's bed, but they began to use it as a couch and left the table standing even when they were not eating. Spring came. Jia Yong's mother stopped talking so much to the cockroach. She did find a small gourd, which she used as the home for the cockroach – whether it was the same or a different one, Yong did not know. At night, sitting in front of the TV, the old lady would hold the gourd close to her face and whisper words that no one could make out.

Jia Yong had announced he would take Hong'er and his mother out to Huairou, a rural county with hiking trails around the Great Wall. The three packed a tin of meat, four boiled eggs, eight steamed buns, a small bag of peanuts, a plastic bottle of orange soda, and four pears. Nie, the Sichuanese with the children's clothing shop, picked them up in his tiny red Alto, and they headed northeast on the old Jingshun Road. Hong'er sat in front with Nie, and Jia Yong sat with his mother in the back.

After about an hour and a half on the road, they arrived

at the base of the Mutianyu section of the wall. Nie led the two women to a mule path next to the parking lots that vendors used to carry cases of soda, postcards, and souvenirs to the top of the wall. Nie did not want to pay the admission fee. He extended his hand to his mother and hauled her up the steep slope at the beginning of the path; Hong'er scampered up without aid. They pushed aside brambles and climbed for about ten minutes, until they reached an open arch at the base of the wall. Once on top of the wall, the walking was easier. Jia Yong took his mother's arm and walked between her and Hong'er, going up and down the curved back of the wall. He imagined horses walking four abreast between the towers and soldiers huddling against the cold.

"I want you to leave," he said to Hong'er. He kept his eyes straight ahead.

"What?"

"You heard me."

They climbed for a time in silence.

Hong'er spat out, "Why would I want to be with you? You're weak. Your brother is gone, and your mother won't live forever. We will have our own apartment and enough money to live on."

"I never wanted my brother gone," Jia Yong said simply. "You did."

"Of course I did. None of you had the courage to do it. What good was he doing, sitting there in his corner all day with that stupid grin?"

"He was my brother."

"That's why you needed me to help you. Jia Yong, you never see these situations clearly. You know that he was a burden to your whole family. Don't you think one cripple is enough? Did you want to be taking care of both of them your whole life?"

"I just want to be alone again. I want you to go back to Hengshui."

A week passed, and Hong'er did not raise the issue. But on the next Saturday, Jia Yong packed her belongings into her small green suitcase and the red, white, and blue plastic bag that she used for the trips to Sichuan.

"I'll take you to the station," he said. Seeing that Jia Yong was determined, Hong'er grew surly. "You will thank me," she said. "Whoever heard of a whole family of cripples? Do you want to live like animals for the rest of your lives? Jia Yong, you are going to miss me and regret this, and it will be too late. Why would I need you? I can marry anyone I like, and you are too slow anyway. I have to do all the thinking for you. You're like a sad little puppy, sitting around hoping Master will notice you. You sicken me. I hope I never see you again."

Jia Yong wordlessly saw her off on the train to Hengshui. Life resumed its former pace. Jia Yong felt he himself was a cockroach, despised by everyone he met, cursed, ugly, but surviving. Weren't cockroaches the oldest unchanged species on earth? Hadn't he heard that they can survive a nuclear blast?

No one in the Jia family spoke again of Hong'er. Jia Yong's mother viewed her as an unfortunate mistake of the type the young are prone to. She sometimes whispered to it at night, but she no longer went on long monologues about poison and reincarnation. The two settled into a routine, Jia Yong going out during the day to his job as a prep cook, returning around six in the evening to cook dinner, eat with his mother and clean up, then go play cards and drink beer with friends who lived nearby. On Saturdays he would play soccer.

The weather grew colder; Jia Yong went out less, since it was so unpleasant to walk through the cold alleys to find his friends. After dinner, he and his mother would watch television together and chat about something inconsequential. Jia Yong's mother would ask him about what had happened at work. He talked about the characters from the restaurant – the fat, domineering chef with fixed opinions, the ethereal French owners, she of gauzy gowns and a distracted air, he compact, dapper, moustachioed, as well as the young waitresses who arrived together before noon and left together around midnight, like a flock of gazelles. His stories about these people delighted his mother, for whom Jia Yong's workmates had a delightful unreality, like characters on a television show, with whom one could not interact. Eight months after Jia Wei's death, they no longer spoke of it.

One Saturday morning, Jia Yong woke first. As he sat up in bed, preparing to go brush his teeth, he became aware that something was different in the room. The door, which he always closed, was ajar, and the wedding photo with the Rolls Royce was missing. Thinking it had fallen off the chest of drawers at night, Jia Yong got up to look in the space between the chest and the wall, and it was then that he noticed that his wallet, which he always left on top of the chest of drawers when he went to bed, was missing. He went out into the main room.

"Ma, did you come into my room last night?" She looked at him in panic, as if caught.

"No, I've been right here."

Jia Yong went to brush his teeth and scrape the

stubble off his chin. He thought he must have moved the wallet and photo and forgotten. But when he opened the refrigerator to get the leftovers from dinner, he saw that the arrangement was unfamiliar. The plastic bottle of Coca-Cola was gone. The green enamel pot that held last night's shredded potato dish had been moved to the back of the top shelf. Jia Yong took the pot out of the refrigerator contemplatively and laid the small folding table with two pairs of chopsticks, the potatoes, and a small dish of peanuts. He knelt down to check on the pressure cooker, in which he was heating porridge.

"She stood in your room," his mother mumbled.

"Who did?"

"She stood in your room. Why didn't she slit your throat?" she whispered hoarsely with frightening conviction. "She comes to look at us."

Jia Yong squatted down by the pressure cooker, opened the lid, and ladled out three bowls of porridge. He crouched on his stool picking up large clumps of the sautéed potato strips with numbing peppercorns seeded through. That afternoon, he bought new locks for the doors and windows.